Sundance
And Other Science Fiction Stories

Sundance
And Other
Science Fiction Stories

by Robert Silverberg

THOMAS NELSON INC.
NASHVILLE / NEW YORK

First edition

Library of Congress Cataloging in Publication Data

Silverberg, Robert.
    Sundance and other science fiction stories.

    SUMMARY: Nine original stories comprise this collection, including "Neutral Planet," "Something Wild Is Loose," and "Passport to Sirius."
    1. Science fiction.   [1. Science fiction.   2. Short stories]
I. Title.
PZ7.S5858Su   [Fic]   74–3343
ISBN 0–8407–6386–7

ACKNOWLEDGMENTS

Sundance copyright © 1969 by Mercury Publications, Inc. Reprinted from *Fantasy & Science Fiction*.
    Neighbor copyright © 1964 by Galaxy Publishing Corporation. Reprinted from *Galaxy*.
    Passport to Sirius copyright © 1958 by Quinn Publishing Company. Reprinted from *If*.
    Caught in the Organ Draft copyright © 1972 by Robert Silverberg. Reprinted from *And Walk Now Gently Through the Fire*, edited by Roger Elwood.
    Neutral Planet copyright © 1957 by Columbia Publications, Inc. Reprinted from *Science Fiction Stories*.
    The Pain Peddlers copyright © 1963 by Galaxy Publishing Corporation. Reprinted from *Galaxy*.
    The Overlord's Thumb copyright © 1957 by Royal Publications, Inc. Reprinted from *Infinity*.
    The Outbreeders copyright © 1959 by King-Size Publications, Inc. Reprinted from *Fantastic Universe*.
    Something Wild Is Loose copyright © 1971 by Robert Silverberg. Reprinted from *The Many Worlds of Science Fiction*, edited by Ben Bova.

Contents

Sundance

Today you liquidated about fifty thousand Eaters in Sector A, and now you are spending an uneasy night. You and Herndon flew east at dawn, with the green-gold sunrise at your backs, and sprayed the neural pellets over a thousand hectares along the Forked River. You flew on into the prairie beyond the river, where the Eaters have already been wiped out, and had lunch sprawled on that thick, soft carpet of grass where the first settlement is expected to rise. Herndon picked some juiceflowers, and you enjoyed half an hour of mild hallucinations. Then, as you headed toward the copter to begin an afternoon of further pellet spraying, he said suddenly, "Tom, how would you feel about this if it turned out that the Eaters weren't just animal pests? That they were *people*, say, with a language and rites and a history and all?"

You thought of how it had been for your own people.

"They aren't," you said.

"Suppose they were. Suppose the Eaters—"

"They aren't. Drop it."

Herndon has this streak of cruelty in him that leads him to ask such questions. He goes for the vulnerabilities; it amuses him. All night now his casual remark has echoed in your mind. Suppose the Eaters . . . Suppose the Eaters . . . Suppose . . . Suppose . . .

You sleep for a while, and dream, and in your dreams you swim through rivers of blood.

Foolishness. A feverish fantasy. You know how important it is to exterminate the Eaters fast, before the settlers get here. They're just animals, and not even harmless animals at that; ecology wreckers is what they are, devourers of oxygen-liberating plants, and they have to go. A few have been saved for zoological study. The rest must be destroyed. Ritual extirpation of undesirable beings, the old, old story. But let's not complicate our job with moral qualms, you tell yourself. Let's not dream of rivers of blood.

The Eaters don't even *have* blood, none that could flow in rivers, anyway. What they have is, well, a kind of lymph that permeates every tissue and transmits nourishment along the interfaces. Waste products go out the same way, osmotically. In terms of process, it's structurally analogous to your own kind of circulatory system, except there's no network of blood vessels hooked to a master pump. The life-stuff just oozes through their bodies, as though they were amoebas or sponges or some other low-phylum form. Yet they're definitely high-phylum in nervous system, digestive setup, limb-and-organ template, etc. Odd, you think. The thing about aliens is that they're alien, you tell yourself, not for the first time.

The beauty of their biology for you and your companions is that it lets you exterminate them so neatly.

You fly over the grazing grounds and drop the neural pellets. The Eaters find and ingest them. Within an hour the poison has reached all sectors of the body. Life ceases; a rapid breakdown of cellular matter follows, the Eaters literally falling apart molecule by molecule the instant that nutrition is cut off; the lymph-like stuff works like acid; a universal lysis occurs; flesh and even the bones, which are cartilaginous, dissolve. In two hours, a puddle on the ground. In four, nothing at all left. Considering how many millions of Eaters you've scheduled for extermination here, it's sweet of the bodies to be self-disposing. Otherwise what a charnel house this world would become!

Suppose the Eaters . . .

Damn Herndon. You almost feel like getting a memory-editing in the morning. Scrape his stupid speculations out of your head. If you dared. If you dared.

In the morning he does not dare. Memory-editing frightens him; he will try to shake free of his new-found guilt without it. The Eaters, he explains to himself, are mindless herbivores, the unfortunate victims of human expansionism, but not really deserving of passionate defense. Their extermination is not tragic; it's just too bad. If Earthmen are to have this world, the Eaters must relinquish it. There's a difference, he tells himself, between the elimination of the Plains Indians from the American prairie in the nineteenth century and the destruction of the bison on that same prairie. One feels a little wistful about the slaughter of the thundering herds; one regrets the butchering of millions of the noble brown woolly beasts, yes. But one feels outrage, not mere wistful regret, at what was done to the Sioux. There's a difference. Reserve your passions for the proper cause.

He walks from his bubble at the edge of the camp toward the center of things. The flagstone path is moist and glistening. The morning fog has not yet lifted, and every tree is bowed, the long, notched leaves heavy with droplets of water. He pauses, crouching, to observe a spider-analog spinning its asymmetrical web. As he watches, a small amphibian, delicately shaded turquoise, glides as inconspicuously as possible over the mossy ground. Not inconspicuously enough; he gently lifts the little creature and puts it on the back of his hand. The gills flutter in anguish, and the amphibian's sides quiver. Slowly, cunningly, its color changes until it matches the coppery tone of the hand. The camouflage is excellent. He lowers his hand and the amphibian scurries into a puddle. He walks on.

He is forty years old, shorter than most of the other members of the expedition, with wide shoulders, a heavy chest, dark glossy hair, a blunt, spreading nose. He is a biologist. This is his third career, for he has failed as an anthropologist and as a developer of real estate. His name is Tom Two Ribbons. He has been married twice but has had no children. His great-grandfather died of alcoholism; his grandfather was addicted to hallucinogens; his father had compulsively visited cheap memory-editing parlors. Tom Two Ribbons is conscious that he is failing a family tradition, but he has not yet found his own mode of self-destruction.

In the main building he discovers Herndon, Julia, Ellen, Schwartz, Chang, Michaelson, and Nichols. They are eating breakfast; the others are already at work. Ellen rises and comes to him and kisses him. Her short soft yellow hair tickles his cheeks. "I love you," she whispers. She has spent the night in Michaelson's bubble. "I love you," he tells her, and draws a quick vertical line of affection between her small pale breasts. He winks at Michaelson, who nods, touches the tops of two fingers to his lips, and blows them a kiss. We are all good friends here, Tom Two Ribbons thinks.

"Who drops pellets today?" he asks.

"Mike and Chang," says Julia. "Sector C."

Schwartz says, "Eleven more days and we ought to have the whole peninsula clear. Then we can move inland."

"If our pellet supply holds up," Chang points out.

Herndon says, "Did you sleep well, Tom?"

"No," says Tom. He sits down and taps out his breakfast requisition. In the west, the fog is beginning to burn off the mountains. Something throbs in the back of his neck. He has been on this world nine weeks now, and in that time it has undergone its only change of season, shading from dry weather to foggy. The mists will remain for many months. Before the plains parch again, the Eaters will be gone and the settlers will begin to arrive. His food slides down the chute and he seizes it. Ellen sits beside him. She is a little more than half his age; this is her first voyage; she is their keeper of records, but she is also skilled at editing. "You look troubled," Ellen tells him. "Can I help you?"

"No. Thank you."

"I hate it when you get gloomy."

"It's a racial trait," says Tom Two Ribbons.

"I doubt that very much."

"The truth is that maybe my personality reconstruct is wearing thin. The trauma level was so close to the surface. I'm just a walking veneer, you know."

Ellen laughs prettily. She wears only a spray-on half-wrap. Her skin looks damp; she and Michaelson have had a swim at dawn. Tom Two Ribbons is thinking of asking her to marry him when this job is over. He has not been married since the collapse of the real estate business. The therapist suggested divorce as part of the reconstruct. He sometimes wonders where Terry has gone and whom she lives with now. Ellen says, "You seem pretty stable to me, Tom."

"Thank you," he says. She is young. She does not know.

"If it's just a passing gloom, I can edit it out in one quick snip."

"Thank you," he says. "No."

"I forgot. You don't like editing."

"My father . . ."

"Yes?"

"In fifty years he pared himself down to a thread," Tom Two Ribbons says. "He had his ancestors edited away, his whole heritage, his religion, his wife, his sons, finally his name. Then he sat and smiled all day. Thank you, no editing."

"Where are you working today?" Ellen asks.

"In the compound, running tests."

"Want company? I'm off all morning."

"Thank you, no," he says, too quickly. She looks hurt. He tries to remedy his unintended cruelty by touching her arm lightly and saying, "Maybe this afternoon, all right? I need to commune a while. Yes?"

"Yes," she says, and smiles, and shapes a kiss with her lips.

After breakfast he goes to the compound. It covers a thousand hectares east of the base; they have bordered it with neural-field projectors at intervals of eighty meters, and this is a sufficient fence to keep the captive population of two hundred Eaters from straying. When all the others have been exterminated, this study group will remain. At the southwest corner of the compound stands a lab bubble from which the experiments are run: metabolic, psychological, physiological, ecological. A stream crosses the compound diagonally. There is a low ridge of grassy hills at its eastern edge. Five distinct copses of tightly clustered knifeblade trees are separated by patches of dense savanna. Sheltered beneath the grass are the oxygen-plants, almost completely hidden except for the photosynthetic spikes that jut to heights of three or four meters at regular intervals, and for the lemon-colored respiratory bodies, chest high, that make the grassland sweet and dizzying with exhaled gases. Through the fields move the Eaters in a straggling herd, nibbling delicately at the respiratory bodies.

Tom Two Ribbons spies the herd beside the stream and

goes toward it. He stumbles over an oxygen-plant hidden in the grass but deftly recovers his balance and, seizing the puckered orifice of the respiratory body, inhales deeply. His despair lifts. He approaches the Eaters. They are spherical, bulky, slow-moving creatures, covered by masses of coarse orange fur. Saucerlike eyes protrude above narrow rubbery lips. Their legs are thin and scaly, like a chicken's, and their arms are short and held close to their bodies. They regard him with bland lack of curiosity. "Good morning, brothers!" is the way he greets them this time, and he wonders why.

I noticed something strange today. Perhaps I simply sniffed too much oxygen in the fields; maybe I was succumbing to a suggestion Herndon planted; or possibly it's the family masochism cropping out. But while I was observing the Eaters in the compound, it seemed to me, for the first time, that they were behaving intelligently, that they were functioning in a ritualized way.

I followed them around for three hours. During that time they uncovered half a dozen outcroppings of oxygen-plants. In each case they went through a stylized pattern of action before starting to munch. They:

Formed a straggly circle around the plants.

Looked toward the sun.

Looked toward their neighbors on left and right around the circle.

Made fuzzy neighing sounds *only* after having done the foregoing.

Looked toward the sun again.

Moved in and ate.

If this wasn't a prayer of thanksgiving, a saying of grace, then what was it? And if they're advanced enough spiritually to say grace, are we not therefore committing genocide here? Do chimpanzees say grace? Christ, we wouldn't even wipe out chimps the way we're cleaning out the Eaters! Of course, chimps don't interfere with human crops, and some kind of coexistence would be possible, whereas Eaters and human agriculturalists simply can't function on the same planet. Nevertheless, there's a moral issue here. The liquidation effort is predicated on the assumption that the intelligence level of the Eaters is about on a par with that of oysters, or, at best, sheep. Our consciences stay clear because our poison is quick and painless and because the Eaters thoughtfully dissolve upon dying, sparing us the mess of incinerating millions of corpses. But if they pray . . .

I won't say anything to the others just yet. I want more evidence, hard, objective. Films, tapes, record cubes. Then we'll see. What if I can show that we're exterminating intelligent beings? My family knows a little about genocide, after all, having been on the receiving end just a few centuries back. I doubt that I could halt what's going on here. But at the very least I could withdraw from the operation. Head back to Earth and stir up public outcries.

I hope I'm imagining this.

I'm not imagining a thing. They gather in circles; they look to the sun; they neigh and pray. They're only balls of jelly on chicken-legs, but they give thanks for their food. Those big round eyes now seem to stare accusingly at me. Our tame herd here knows what's going on: that we have descended from the stars to eradicate their kind, and that they alone will be spared. They have no way of fighting back or even of communicating their displeasure, but they *know*. And hate us. Jesus, we have killed two million of them since we got here, and in a metaphorical way I'm stained with blood, and what will I do, what can I do?

I must move very carefully, or I'll end up drugged and edited.

I can't let myself seem like a crank, a quack, an agitator. I can't stand up and *denounce!* I have to find allies. Herndon, first. He surely is on to the truth; he's the one who nudged *me* to it, that day we dropped pellets. And I thought he was merely being vicious in his usual way!

I'll talk to him tonight.

He says, "I've been thinking about that suggestion you made. About the Eaters. Perhaps we haven't made sufficiently close psychological studies. I mean, if they really *are* intelligent . . ."

Herndon blinks. He is a tall man with glossy dark hair, a heavy beard, sharp cheekbones. "Who says they are, Tom?"

"You did. On the far side of the Forked River, you said—"

"It was just a speculative hypothesis. To make conversation."

"No, I think it was more than that. You really believed it."

Herndon looks troubled. "Tom, I don't know what you're trying to start, but don't start it. If I for a moment believed we were killing intelligent creatures, I'd run for an editor so fast I'd start an implosion wave."

"Why did you ask me that thing, then?" Tom Two Ribbons says.

"Idle chatter."

"Amusing yourself by kindling guilts in somebody else? You're a bastard, Herndon. I mean it."

"Well, look, Tom, if I had any idea that you'd get so worked up about a hypothetical suggestion . . ." Herndon shakes his head. "The Eaters aren't intelligent beings. Obviously. Otherwise we wouldn't be under orders to liquidate them."

"Obviously," says Tom Two Ribbons.

Ellen said, "No, I don't know what Tom's up to. But I'm pretty sure he needs a rest. It's only a year and a half since his personality reconstruct, and he had a pretty bad breakdown back then."

Michaelson consulted a chart. "He's refused three times in a row to make his pellet-dropping run. Claiming he can't take time away from his research. Hell, we can fill in for him, but it's the idea that he's ducking chores that bothers me."

"What kind of research is he doing?" Nichols wanted to know.

"Not biological," said Julia. "He's with the Eaters in the compound all the time, but I don't see him making any tests on them. He just watches them."

"And talks to them," Chang observed.

"And talks, yes," Julia said.

"About what?" Nichols asked.

"Who knows?"

Everyone looked at Ellen. "You're closest to him," Michaelson said. "Can't you bring him out of it?"

"I've got to know what he's in, first," Ellen said. "He isn't saying a thing."

You know that you must be very careful, for they outnumber you, and their concern for your mental welfare can be deadly. Already they realize you are disturbed, and Ellen has begun to probe for the source of the disturbance. Last night you lay in her arms and she questioned you, obliquely, skillfully, and you knew what she is trying to find out. When the moons appeared she suggested that you and she stroll in the compound, among the sleeping Eaters. You declined, but she sees that you have become involved with the creatures.

You have done probing of your own—subtly, you hope. And you are aware that you can do nothing to save the Eaters. An irrevocable commitment has been made. It is 1876 all over again; these are the bison, these are the Sioux, and they must be destroyed, for the railroad is on its way. If you speak out here, your friends will calm you and pacify you and edit you, for they do not see what you see. If you return to Earth to agitate, you will be mocked and recommended for another reconstruct. You can do nothing. You can do nothing.

You cannot save, but perhaps you can record.

Go out into the prairie. Live with the Eaters; make yourself their friend; learn their ways. Set it down, a full account of their culture, so that at least that much will not be lost. You know the techniques of field anthropology. As was done for your people in the old days, do now for the Eaters.

He finds Michaelson. "Can you spare me for a few weeks?" he asks.

"Spare you, Tom? What do you mean?"

"I've got some field studies to do. I'd like to leave the base and work with Eaters in the wild."

"What's wrong with the ones in the compound?"

"It's the last chance with wild ones, Mike. I've got to go."

"Alone, or with Ellen?"

"Alone."

Michaelson nods slowly. "All right, Tom. Whatever you want. Go. I won't hold you here."

I dance in the prairie under the green-gold sun. About

me the Eaters gather. I am stripped; sweat makes my
skin glisten; my heart pounds. I talk to them with my
feet, and they understand.

They understand.

They have a language of soft sounds. They have a
god. They know love and awe and rapture. They have
rites. They have names. They have a history. Of all
this I am convinced.

I dance on thick grass.

How can I reach them? With my feet, with my hands,
with my grunts, with my sweat. They gather by the hundreds, by the thousands, and I dance. I must not
stop. They cluster about me and make their sounds. I am
a conduit for strange forces. My great-grandfather
should see me now! Sitting on his porch in Wyoming, the
firewater in his hand, his brain rotting—see me now; old
one! See the dance of Tom Two Ribbons! I talk to these
strange ones with my feet under a sun that is the wrong
color. I dance. I dance.

"Listen to me," I say. "I am your friend, I alone, the
only one you can trust. Trust me, talk to me, teach me.
Let me preserve your ways, for soon the destruction
will come."

I dance, and the sun climbs, and the Eaters murmur.

There is the chief. I dance toward him, back, toward, I
bow, I point to the sun, I imagine the being that lives in
that ball of flame, I imitate the sounds of these people,
I kneel, I rise, I dance. Tom Two Ribbons dances for
you.

I summon skills my ancestors forgot. I feel the power
flowing in me. As they danced in the days of the bison, I
dance now, beyond the Forked River.

I dance, and now the Eaters dance too. Slowly, uncertainly, they move toward me, they shift their weight, lift
leg and leg, sway about. "Yes, like that!" I cry. "Dance!"

We dance together as the sun reaches noon height.

Now their eyes are no longer accusing. I see warmth and kinship. I am their brother, their red-skinned tribesman, he who dances with them. No longer do they seem clumsy to me. There is a strange ponderous grace in their movements. They dance. They dance. They caper about me. Closer, closer, closer!

We move in holy frenzy.

They sing, now, a blurred hymn of joy. They throw forth their arms, unclench their little claws. In unison they shift weight, left foot forward, right, left, right. Dance, brothers, dance, dance, dance! They press against me. Their flesh quivers; their smell is a sweet one. They gently thrust me across the field, to a part of the meadow where the grass is deep and untrampled. Still dancing, we seek for the oxygen-plants, and find clumps of them beneath the grass, and they make their prayer and seize them with their awkward arms, separating the respiratory bodies from the photosynthetic spikes. The plants, in anguish, release floods of oxygen. My mind reels. I laugh and sing. The Eaters are nibbling the lemon-colored perforated globes, nibbling the stalks as well. They thrust their plants at me. It is a religious ceremony, I see. Take from us, eat with us, join with us, this is the body, this is the blood, take, eat, join. I bend forward and put a lemon-colored globe to my lips. I do not bite; I nibble, as they do, my teeth slicing away the skin of the globe. Juice spurts into my mouth, while oxygen drenches my nostrils. The Eaters sing hosannas. I should be in full paint for this, paint of my forefathers, feathers too, meeting their religion in the regalia of what should have been mine. Take, eat, join. The juice of the oxygen-plant flows in my veins. I embrace my brothers. I sing, and as my voice leaves my lips it becomes an arch that glistens like new steel, and I pitch my song lower, and the arch turns to tarnished silver. The Eaters crowd close. The scent of their bodies is fiery red to me. Their soft cries are puffs of steam. The sun is very warm; its rays are tiny jagged pings of puckered sound, close to the top of my range of hearing, plink! plink! plink! The thick grass hums to me, deep and rich, and the wind hurls points of flame along the prairie. I devour another oxygen-plant, and then a third. My brothers laugh and shout. They tell me of their gods, the god of warmth, the god of food, the god of pleasure, the god of death, the god of holiness, the god of wrongness, and the others. They recite for me the names of their kings, and I hear their voices as splashes of green mold on the clean sheet of the sky. They instruct me in their holy rites. I must remember this, I tell myself, for when it is gone it will never come again. I continue to dance. They continue to dance. The color of the hills becomes rough and coarse, like abrasive gas. Take, eat, join. Dance. They are so gentle!

I hear the drone of the copter, suddenly.

It hovers far overhead. I am unable to see who flies in it. "No," I scream. "Not here! Not these people! Listen to me! This is Tom Two Ribbons! Can't you hear me? I'm doing a field study here! You have no right—!"

My voice makes spirals of blue moss edged with red sparks. They drift upward and are scattered by the breeze.

I yell, I shout, I bellow. I dance and shake my fists. From the wings of the copter the jointed arms of the pellet-distributors unfold. The gleaming spigots extend and whirl. The neural pellets rain down into the meadow, each tracing a blazing track that lingers in the sky. The sound of the copter becomes a furry carpet stretching to the horizon, and my shrill voice is lost in it.

The Eaters drift away from me, seeking the pellets,

scratching at the roots of the grass to find them. Still dancing, I leap into their midst, striking the pellets from their hands, hurling them into the stream, crushing them to powder. The Eaters growl black needles at me. They turn away and search for more pellets. The copter turns and flies off, leaving a trail of dense oily sound. My brothers are gobbling the pellets eagerly.

There is no way to prevent it.

Joy consumes them and they topple and lie still. Occasionally a limb twitches; then even this stops. They begin to dissolve. Thousands of them melt on the prairie, sinking into shapelessness, losing their spherical forms, flattening, ebbing into the ground. The bonds of the molecules will no longer hold. It is the twilight of protoplasm. They perish. They vanish. For hours I walk the prairie. Now I inhale oxygen; now I eat a lemon-colored globe. Sunset begins with the ringing of leaden chimes. Black clouds make brazen trumpet calls in the east and the deepening wind is a swirl of coaly bristles. Silence comes. Night falls. I dance. I am alone.

The copter comes again, and they find you, and you do not resist as they gather you in. You are beyond bitterness. Quietly you explain what you have done and what you have learned, and why it is wrong to exterminate these people. You describe the plant you have eaten and the way it affects your senses, and as you talk of the blessed synesthesia, the texture of the wind and the sound of the clouds and the timbre of the sunlight, they nod and smile and tell you not to worry, that everything will be all right soon, and they touch something cold to your forearm, so cold that it is a whir and a buzz and the deintoxicant sinks into your vein and soon the ecstasy drains away, leaving only the exhaustion and the grief.

He says, "We never learn a thing, do we? We export all

our horrors to the stars. Wipe out the Armenians, wipe out the Jews, wipe out the Tasmanians, wipe out the Indians, wipe out everyone who's in the way, and then come out here and do the same damned murderous thing. You weren't with me out there. You didn't dance with them. You didn't see what a rich, complex culture the Eaters have. Let me tell you about their tribal structure. It's dense: seven levels of matrimonial relationships, to begin with, and an exogamy factor that requires—"

Softly Ellen says, "Tom, darling, nobody's going to harm the Eaters."

"And the religion," he goes on. "Nine gods, each one an aspect of *the* god. Holiness and wrongness both worshiped. They have hymns, prayers, a theology. And we, the emissaries of the god of wrongness—"

"We're not exterminating them," Michaelson says. "Won't you understand that, Tom? This is all a fantasy of yours. You've been under the influence of drugs, but now we're clearing you out. You'll be clean in a little while. You'll have perspective again."

"A fantasy?" he says bitterly. "A drug dream? I stood out in the prairie and saw you drop pellets. And I watched them die and melt away. I didn't dream that."

"How can we convince you?" Chang asks earnestly. "What will make you believe? Shall we fly over the Eater country with you and show you how many millions there are?"

"But how many millions have been destroyed?" he demands.

They insist that he is wrong. Ellen tells him again that no one has ever desired to harm the Eaters. "This is a scientific expedition, Tom. We're here to *study* them. It's a violation of all we stand for to injure intelligent lifeforms."

"You admit that they're intelligent?"

"Of course. That's never been in doubt."

"Then why drop the pellets?" he asks. "Why slaughter them?"

"None of that has happened, Tom," Ellen says. She takes his hand between her cool palms. "Believe us. Believe us."

He says bitterly, "If you want me to believe you, why don't you do the job properly? Get out the editing machine and go to work on me. You can't simply *talk* me into rejecting the evidence of my own eyes."

"You were under drugs all the time," Michaelson says.

"I've never taken drugs! Except for what I ate in the meadow, when I danced—and that came after I had watched the massacre going on for weeks and weeks. Are you saying that it's a retroactive delusion?"

"No, Tom," Schwartz says. "You've had this delusion all along. It's part of your therapy, your reconstruct. You came here programmed with it."

"Impossible," he says.

Ellen kisses his fevered forehead. "It was done to reconcile you to mankind, you see. You had this terrible resentment of the displacement of your people in the nineteenth century. You were unable to forgive the industrial society for scattering the Sioux, and you were terribly full of hate. Your therapist thought that if you could be made to participate in an imaginary modern extermination, if you could come to see it as a necessary operation, you'd be purged of your resentment and able to take your place in society as—"

He thrusts her away. "Don't talk idiocy! If you knew the first thing about reconstruct therapy, you'd realize that no reputable therapist could be so shallow. There are no one-to-one correlations in reconstructs. No, don't touch me. Keep away. Keep away."

He will not let them persuade him that this is merely a

drug-borne dream. It is no fantasy, he tells himself, and it is no therapy. He rises. He goes out. They do not follow him. He takes a copter and seeks his brothers.

Again I dance. The sun is much hotter today. The Eaters are more numerous. Today I wear paint, today I wear feathers. My body shines with my sweat. They dance with me, and they have a frenzy in them that I have never seen before. We pound the trampled meadow with our feet. We clutch for the sun with our hands. We sing, we shout, we cry. We will dance until we fall.

This is no fantasy. These people are real, and they are intelligent, and they are doomed. This I know.

We dance. Despite the doom, we dance.

My great-grandfather comes and dances with us. He, too, is real. His nose is like a hawk's, not blunt like mine, and he wears the big headdress, and his muscles are cords under his brown skin. He sings, he shouts, he cries.

Others of my family join us.

We eat the oxygen-plants together. We embrace the Eaters. We know, all of us, what it is to be hunted.

The clouds make music and the wind takes on texture and the sun's warmth has color.

We dance. We dance. Our limbs know no weariness.

The sun grows and fills the whole sky, and I see no Eaters now, only my own people, my father's fathers across the centuries, thousands of gleaming skins, thousands of hawks' noses, and we eat the plants, and we find sharp sticks and thrust them into our flesh, and the sweet blood flows and dries in the blaze of the sun, and we dance, and we dance, and some of us fall from weariness, and we dance, and the prairie is a sea of bobbing headdresses, an ocean of feathers, and we dance, and my heart makes thunder, and my knees become water, and the sun's fire engulfs me, and I dance, and I fall, and I dance, and I fall, and I fall, and I fall.

Again they find you and bring you back. They give you the cool snout on your arm to take the oxygen-plant drug from your veins, and then they give you something else so you will rest. You rest and you are very calm. Ellen kisses you and you stroke her soft skin, and then the others come in and they talk to you, saying soothing things, but you do not listen, for you are searching for realities. It is not an easy search. It is like falling through many trap-doors, looking for the one room whose floor is not hinged. Everything that has happened on this planet is your therapy, you tell yourself, designed to reconcile an embittered aborigine to the white man's conquest; nothing is really being exterminated here. You reject that and fall through and realize that this must be the therapy of your friends; they carry the weight of accumulated centuries of guilts and have come here to shed that load, and you are here to ease them of their burden, to draw their sins into yourself and give them forgiveness. Again you fall through, and see that the Eaters are mere animals who threaten the ecology and must be removed; the culture you imagined for them is your hallucination, kindled out of old churnings. You try to withdraw your objections to this necessary extermination, but you fall through again and discover that there is no extermination except in your mind, which is troubled and disordered by your obsession with the crime against your ancestors, and you sit up, for you wish to apologize to these friends of yours, these innocent scientists whom you have called murderers. And you fall through.

Neighbor

Fresh snow had fallen during the night. It lay like a white sheet atop the older snow, nine or ten feet of it, that already covered the plain. Now all was smooth and clear almost to the horizon. As Michael Holt peered through the foot-thick safety glass of his command-room window, he saw, first of all, the zone of brown earth, a hundred yards in diameter, circling his house, and then the beginning of the snowfield with a few jagged bare trees jutting through it, and then, finally, a blot on the horizon, the metallic tower that was Andrew McDermott's dwelling.

Not in seventy or eighty years had Holt looked at the McDermott place without feeling hatred and irritation. The planet was big enough, wasn't it? Why had McDermott chosen to stick his pile of misshapen steel down right where Holt had to look at it all his days? The McDermott estate was large. McDermott could have built his house another fifty or sixty miles to the east, near the banks of the wide, shallow river that flowed through the heart of the continent. He hadn't cared to. Holt had politely suggested it, when the surveyors and architects first came out from Earth. McDermott had just as politely insisted on putting his house where he wanted to put it.

It was still there. Michael Holt peered at it, and his insides roiled. He walked to the control console of the armament panel, and let his thin, gnarled hands rest for a moment on a gleaming rheostat.

There was an almost sexual manner to the way Holt

fondled the jutting knobs and studs of the console. Now that his two-hundredth year was approaching, he rarely handled the bodies of his wives that way anymore. But, then, he did not love his wives as keenly as he loved the artillery emplacement with which he could blow Andrew McDermott to atoms.

Just let him provoke me, Holt thought.

He stood by the panel, a tall, gaunt man with a withered face and a savage hook of a nose and a surprisingly thick shock of faded red hair. He closed his eyes and allowed himself the luxury of a daydream.

He imagined that Andrew McDermott had given him offense. Not simply the eternal offense of being there in his view, but some direct, specific affront. Poaching on his land, perhaps. Or sending a robot out to hack down a tree on the borderland. Or putting up a flashing neon sign mocking Holt in some vulgar way. Anything that would serve as an excuse for hostilities.

And then: Holt saw himself coming up here to the command room and broadcasting an ultimatum to the enemy. "Take that sign down, McDermott," he might say. "Keep your robots off my land," perhaps. "Or else this means war."

McDermott would reply with a blast of radiation, of course, because that was the kind of sneak he was. The deflector screens of Holt's front-line defenses would handle the bolt with ease, soaking it in and feeding the energy straight to Holt's own generators.

Then, at long last, Holt would answer back. His fingers would tighten on the controls. Crackling arcs of energy would leap toward the ionosphere and bound downward at McDermott's place, spearing through his pitiful screens as though they weren't there. Holt saw himself gripping the controls with knuckle-whitening fervor, launching thunderbolt after thunderbolt, while on the horizon Andrew McDermott's hideous keep blazed and glowed in hellish fire, and crumpled and toppled and ran in molten puddles over the snow.

Yes, that would be the moment to live for!

That would be the moment of triumph!

To step back from the controls at last and look through the window and see the glowing red spot on the horizon where the McDermott place had been. To pat the controls as though they were the flanks of a beloved old horse. To leave the house, and ride across the borderland into the McDermott estate, and see the charred ruin, and know that he was gone forever.

Then, of course, there would be an inquiry. The fifty lords of the planet would meet to discuss the battle, and Holt would explain, "He wantonly provoked me. I need not tell you how he gave me offense by building his house within my view. But this time—"

And Holt's fellow lords would nod sagely, and would understand, for they valued their own unblemished views as highly as Holt himself. They would exonerate him and grant him McDermott's land, as far as the horizon, so no newcomer could repeat the offense.

Michael Holt smiled. The daydream left him satisfied. His heart raced perhaps a little too enthusiastically as he pictured the slagheap on the horizon. He made an effort to calm himself. He was, after all, a fragile old man, much as he hated to admit it, and even the excitement of a daydream taxed his strength.

He walked away from the panel, back to the window. Nothing had changed. The zone of brown earth where his melters kept back the snow, and then the white field, and finally the excrescence on the horizon, glinting coppery red in the thin midday sunlight. Holt scowled. The daydream had changed nothing. No shot had been fired.

McDermott's keep still stained the view. Turning, Holt began to shuffle slowly out of the room, toward the dropshaft that would take him five floors downward to his family.

The communicator chimed. Holt stared at the screen in surprise.

"Yes?"

"An outside call for you, Lord Holt. Lord McDermott is calling," the bland metallic voice said.

"Lord McDermott's secretary, you mean."

"It is Lord McDermott himself, your lordship."

Holt blinked. "You're joking," he said. "It's fifty years since he called me. If this is a prank, I'll have your circuits shorted!"

"I cannot joke, your lordship. Shall I tell Lord McDermott you do not wish to speak to him?"

"Of course," Holt snapped. "No . . . wait. Find out what he wants. *Then* tell him I can't speak to him."

Holt sank back into a chair in front of the screen. He nudged a button with his elbow, and tiny hands began to massage the muscles of his back, where tension-poisons had suddenly flooded in to stiffen him.

McDermott calling? What for?

To complain, of course. Some trespass, no doubt. Some serious trespass, if McDermott felt he had to make the call himself. Michael Holt's blood warmed. Let him complain! Let him accuse, let him bluster! Perhaps this would give the excuse for hostilities at last. Holt ached to declare war. He had been building his armaments patiently for decade after decade, and he knew beyond doubt that he had the capability to destroy McDermott moments after the first shot was fired. No screens in the universe could withstand the array of weaponry Holt had assembled. The outcome of a conflict was in no doubt.

Let him start something, Michael Holt prayed. *Oh, let him be the aggressor! I'm ready for him, and more than ready!*

The bell chimed again. The robot voice of Holt's secretary said, "I have spoken to him, your lordship. He will tell me nothing. He wants to speak to you."

Holt sighed. "Very well. Put him on, then."

There was a moment of electronic chaos on the screen as the robot shifted from the inside channel to an outside one. Holt sat stiffly, annoyed by the sudden anxiety he felt. He realized, strangely, that he had forgotten what his enemy's voice sounded like. All communication between them had been through robot intermediaries for years.

The screen brightened and showed a test pattern. A hoarse, querulous voice said, "Holt? Holt, where are you?"

"Right here in my chair, McDermott. What's troubling you?"

"Turn your vision on. Let me have a look at you, Holt."

"You can speak your piece without seeing me, can't you? Is my face that fascinating to you?"

"Please. This is no time for bickering. Turn the vision on!"

"Let me remind you," Holt said coldly, "that *you* have called *me*. The normal rules of etiquette require that I have the privilege of deciding on the manner of transmission. And I prefer not to be seen. I also prefer not to be speaking to you. You have thirty seconds to state your complaint. Important business awaits me."

There was silence. Holt gripped the arms of his chair and signaled for a more intense massage. He became aware, in great irritation, that his hands were trembling. He glared at the screen as though he could burn his enemy's brain out simply by sending angry thoughts over the communicator.

McDermott said finally, "I have no complaint, Holt. Only an invitation."

"To tea?"

"Call it that. I want you to come here, Holt."

"You've lost your mind!"

"Not yet. Come to me. Let's have a truce," McDermott rasped. "We're both old, sick, stupid men. It's time to stop the hatred."

Holt laughed. "We're both old, yes. But I'm not sick and you're the only stupid one. Isn't it a little late for the olive branch?"

"Never too late."

"You know there can't ever be peace between us," Holt said. "Not so long as that eyesore of yours sticks up over the trees. It's a cinder in my eye, McDermott. I can't ever forgive you for building it."

"Will you listen to me?" McDermott said. "When I'm gone, you can blast the place apart, if it pleases you. All I want is for you to come here. I—I need you, Holt. I want you to pay me a visit."

"Why don't you come here, then?" Holt jeered. "I'll throw my door wide for you. We'll sit by the fire and reminisce about all the years we hated each other."

"If I could come to you," McDermott said, "there would be no need for us to meet at all."

"What do you mean?"

"Turn your visual on, and you'll see."

Michael Holt frowned. He knew he had become hideous with age, and he was not eager to show himself to his enemy. But he could not see McDermott without revealing himself at the same time. With an abrupt, impulsive gesture, Holt jabbed the control button in his chair. The mists on the screen faded, and an image appeared.

All Holt could see was a face, shrunken, wizened,

wasted. McDermott was past two hundred, Holt knew, and he looked it. There was no flesh left on his face. The skin lay like parchment over bone. The left side of his face was distorted, the nostril flared, the mouth corner dragged down to reveal the teeth, the eyelid drooping. Below the chin, McDermott was invisible, swathed in machinery, his body cocooned in what was probably a nutrient bath. He was obviously in bad shape.

He said, "I've had a stroke, Holt. I'm paralyzed from the neck down. I can't hurt you."

"When did this happen?"

"A year ago."

"You've kept very quiet about it," Holt said.

"I didn't think you'd care to know. But now I do. I'm dying, Holt, and I want to see you once face to face before I die. I know, you're suspicious. You think I'm crazy to ask you to come here. Well, maybe I am crazy. I'll turn my screens off. I'll send all my robots across the river. I'll be absolutely alone here, helpless, and you can come with an army if you like. There. Doesn't that sound like a trap, Holt? I know I'd think so if I were in your place and you were in mine. But it isn't a trap. Can you believe that? I'll open my door to you. You can come and laugh in my face as I lie here. But come. There's something I have to tell you, something of vital importance to you. And you've got to be here in person when I tell you. You won't regret coming. Believe that, Holt."

Holt stared at the wizened creature on the screen, and trembled with doubt and confusion. The man must be a lunatic! It was years since Holt had last stepped beyond the protection of his own screens. Now McDermott was asking him not only to go into the open field, where he might be gunned down with ease, but to enter into McDermott's house itself, to put his head right between the jaws of the lion.

Absurd!

McDermott said, "Let me show you my sincerity. My screens are off. Take a shot at the house. Hit it anywhere. Go ahead. Do your worst!"

Deeply troubled, chilled with mystification, Holt elbowed out of his chair, went beyond the range of the visual pickup, over to the control console of the guns. How many times in dreams he had fondled these studs and knobs, never firing them once, except in test shots directed at his own property! It was unreal to be actually training the sights on the gleaming tower of McDermott's house at last. Excitement surged in him. Could this all be some subtle way, he wondered, of causing him to have a fatal heart attack through overstimulation?

He gripped the controls. He pondered, considered tossing a thousand megawatt beam at McDermott, then decided to use something a little milder. If the screens really were down all the way, even his feeblest shot would score.

He sighted—not on the house itself, but on a tree just within McDermott's inner circle of defense. He fired, still half convinced he was dreaming. The tree became a yard-high stump.

"That's it," McDermott called. "Go on. Aim at the house, too. Knock a turret off. The screens are down."

Senile dementia, Holt thought. Baffled, he lifted the sight a bit and let the beam play against one of McDermott's outbuildings. The shielded wall glowed a moment, then gave as the beam smashed its way through. Ten square feet of McDermott's castle now was a soup of protons, fleeing into the cold.

Holt realized in stunned disbelief that there was nothing at all preventing him from destroying McDermott and his odious house entirely. There was no risk of a counterattack. He would not even need to use the heavy artillery that he had been so jealously hoarding against this day. A light beam would do it easily enough.

It would be too easy this way, though.

There could be no pleasure in a wanton attack. McDermott had not provoked him. Rather, he sat there in his cocoon, sniveling and begging to be visited.

Holt returned to the visual field. "I must be as crazy as you are," he said. "Turn your robots loose and leave your screens down. I'll come to visit you. I wish I understood this, but I'll come anyway."

Michael Holt called his family together. Three wives, the eldest near his own age, the youngest only seventy. Seven sons, ranging in age from sixty to a hundred thirteen. The wives of his sons. His grandchildren. His top echelon of robots.

He assembled them in the grand hall of Holt Keep, and took his place at the head of the table, and stared down the rows at their faces, so like his own, and said quietly, "I am going to pay a call on Lord McDermott."

He could see the shock on their faces. They were too well disciplined to speak their minds, of course. He was Lord Holt, and his word was law, and he could, if he so pleased, order them all put to death on the spot. Once, many years before, he had been forced to assert his parental authority in just such a way, and no one would ever forget it.

He smiled. "You think I've gone soft in my old age, and perhaps I have. But McDermott has had a stroke. He's completely paralyzed from the neck down. He wants to tell me something, and I'm going to go. His screens are down and he's sending all his robots out of the house. I could have blasted the place apart if I wanted to."

He could see the muscles working in the jaws of his sons. They wanted to cry out, but they did not dare.

Holt went on, "I'm going alone except for a few robots. If there's been no word from me for half an hour after I'm seen entering the house, you're authorized to come after me. If there's any interference with the rescue party, it will mean war. But I don't think there'll be trouble. Anyone who comes after me in less than half an hour will be put to death."

Holt's words died away in a shiver of echoes. He eyed them all, one at a time. This was a critical moment, he knew. If they dared, they might decide among themselves that he had gone mad, and depose him. That had happened before too, in other families. They could topple him, reprogram all the robots to take commands from them instead, and confine him to his wing of the house. He had given them evidence enough, just now, of his irresponsibility.

But they made no move. They lacked the guts. He was head of the household, and his word was law. They sat, pale and shaken and dazed, as he rolled his chair past them and out of the grand hall.

Within an hour, he was ready to go. Winter was in the fourth of its seven months, and Michael Holt had not left the house since the first snowfall. But he had nothing to fear from the elements. He would not come in contact with the frigid air of the sub-zero plain. He entered his car within his own house, and it glided out past the defense perimeter, a gleaming dark teardrop sliding over the fresh snow. Eight of his robots accompanied him, a good enough army for almost any emergency.

A visual pickup showed him the scene at McDermott Keep. The robots were filing out, an army of black ants clustering around the great gate. He could see them marching eastward, vanishing from sight beyond the house. A robot overhead reported that they were heading for the river by the dozens.

The miles flew past. Black, twisted trees poked through the snow, and Holt's car weaved a way through them. Far below, under many feet of whiteness, lay the fertile fields. In the spring, all would be green, and the leafy trees would help to shield the view of McDermott Keep, though they could not hide it altogether. In winter, the ugly copper-colored house was totally visible. That made the winters all the more difficult for Holt to endure.

A robot said softly, "We are approaching the borderlands, your lordship."

"Try a test shot. See if his screens are still down."

"Shall I aim for the house?"

"No. A tree just in front of it."

Holt watched. A thick-boled, stubby tree in McDermott's front palisade gleamed a moment, and then was not there.

"The screens are still down," the robot reported.

"All right. Let's cross the border."

He leaned back against the cushion. The car shot forward. They left the bounds of Holt's own estate, now, and entered McDermott's. There was no warning ping to tell them they were trespassing. McDermott had even turned off the boundary scanners, then. Holt pressed sweaty palms together. More than ever he felt that he had let himself be drawn into some sort of trap. There was no turning back, now. He was across the border, into McDermott's own territory. Better to die boldly, he thought, than to live huddled in a shell.

He had never been this close to McDermott Keep before. When it was being built, McDermott had invited him to inspect it, but Holt had of course refused. Nor had he been to the housewarming; alone among the lords of the planet, he had stayed home to sulk. He could hardly even remember when he had last left his own land at all. There were few places to go on this world, with its fifty estates of great size running through the temperate belt, and whenever Holt thirsted for the companionship of his fellow lords, which was not often, he could have it easily enough via telescreen. Some of them came to him, now and then. It was strange that when he finally did stir to pay a call, it should be a call on McDermott.

Drawing near the enemy keep, he found himself reluctantly admitting that it was less ugly at close range than it seemed from the windows of Holt Keep. It was a great blocky building, hundreds of yards long, with a tall octagonal tower rising out of its northern end, a metal spike jabbing perhaps five hundred feet high. The reflected afternoon light, bouncing from the snowfield, gave the metal-sheathed building a curiously oily look, not unattractive at this distance.

"We are within the outer defense perimeter," a robot told Holt.

"Fine. Keep going."

The robots sounded worried and perturbed, he thought. Of course, they weren't programmed to show much emotional range, but he could detect a note of puzzlement in what they said and how they said it. They couldn't understand this at all. It did not seem to be an invasion of McDermott Keep—that they could understand—but yet it was not a friendly visit, either. The robots did not know what to make out of this journey.

They were not alone in their confusion, Holt thought grimly.

When they were a hundred yards from the great gate of McDermott Keep, the doors swung open. Holt called McDermott and said, "See that those doors stay open all the time I'm here. If they begin to close, there'll be trouble."

"Don't worry," McDermott said. "I'm not planning any tricks."

Holt's car shot between the gate walls, and he knew that now he was at his enemy's mercy in earnest. His car rolled up to the open carport and went on through, so that now he was actually within McDermott Keep. His robots followed him through.

"May I close the carport?" McDermott asked.

"Keep it open," Holt said. "I don't mind the cold."

The hood of his car swung back. His robots helped him out. Holt shivered momentarily as the cold outside air, filtering into the carport, touched him. Then he passed through the rising inner door, and, flanked by two sturdy robots, walked slowly but doggedly into the Keep.

McDermott's voice reached him over a loudspeaker. "I am on the third floor of the tower," he said. "If I had not sent all the robots away, I could have let one of them guide you."

"You could send a member of your family down," Holt said sourly.

McDermott ignored that. "Continue down the corridor until it turns. Go past the armor room. You will reach a dropshaft that leads upward."

Holt and his robots moved through the silent halls. The place was like a museum, he thought. The dark, high-vaulted corridor was lined with statuary and arti-facts, everything musty-looking and depressing. How could anyone want to live in a tomb like this? Holt passed a shadowy room where ancient suits of armor stood mounted. He could not help but compute the cost of shipping such useless things across the light-years from Earth.

They came to the dropshaft. Holt and his two robots entered. A robot nudged the reversing stud and up they went, into the tower Holt had hated so long. McDermott guided them with a word or two.

They passed down a long hall whose dull, dark walls were set off by a gleaming floor that looked like onyx. A sphincter opened, admitting them to an oval room ringed by windows. There was a dry, foul stench of death and decay in the room. Andrew McDermott sat squarely in the middle of the room, nesting in his life-capsule. A tangled network of tubes and pipes surrounded him. All of McDermott that was visible was a pair of eyes, like shining coals in the wasted face.

"I'm glad you came," McDermott said. His voice, without benefit of electronic amplification, was thin and feeble, like the sound of feathers brushing through the air.

Holt stared at him in fascination. "I never thought I'd see this room," he said.

"I never thought you would either. But it was good of you to come, Holt. You look well, you know. For a man your age." The thin lips curled in a grotesque twisted smile. "Of course, you're still a youngster. Not even two hundred, yet. I've got you by thirty years."

Holt did not feel like listening to the older man's ramblings. "What is it you wanted?" he asked without warmth. "I'm here, but I'm not going to stay all day. You said you had something vital to tell me."

"Not really to tell," McDermott said. "More to ask. A favor. I want you to kill me, Holt."

"What?"

"It's very simple. Disconnect my feed line. There it is, right by my feet. Just rip it out. I'll be dead in an hour. Or do it even more quickly. Turn off my lungs. This switch, right here. That would be the humane way to do it."

"You have a strange sense of humor," Holt said.

"Do you think so? Top the joke, then. Throw the switch and cap the jest."

"You made me come all the way here to *kill* you?"

"Yes," McDermott said. The blazing eyes were unblinking now. "I've been immobilized for a year, now. I'm a vegetable in this thing. I sit here day after day, idle, bored. And healthy. I might live another hundred years, do you realize that, Holt? I've had a stroke, yes. I'm paralyzed. But my body's still vigorous. This damned capsule of mine keeps me in tone. It feeds me and exercises me and—do you think I want to go on living this way, Holt? Would you?"

Holt shrugged. "If you want to die, you could ask someone in your family to unplug you."

"I have no family."

"Is that true? You had five sons . . ."

"Four dead, Holt. The other one gone to Earth. No one lives here any more. I've outlasted them all. I'm as eternal as the heavens. Two hundred thirty years, that's long enough to live. My wives are dead, my grandchildren gone away. They'll come home when they find they've inherited. Not before. There's no one here to throw the switch."

"Your robots," Holt suggested.

Again the grim smile. "You must have special robots, Holt. I don't have any that can be tricked into killing their master. I've tried it. They know what'll happen if my life-capsule is disconnected. They won't do it. *You* do it, Holt. Turn me off. Blow the tower to hell, if it bothers you. You've won the game. The prize is yours."

There was a dryness in Holt's throat, a band of pressure across his chest. He tottered a little. His robots, ever sensitive to his condition, steadied him and guided him to a chair. He had been on his feet a long time for a man of his age. He sat quietly until the spasm passed.

Then he said, "I won't do it."

"Why not?"

"It's too simple, McDermott. I've hated you too long. I can't just flip a switch and turn you off."

"Bombard me, then. Blast the tower down."

"Without provocation? Do you think I'm a criminal?" Holt asked.

"What do you want me to do?" McDermott said tiredly. "Order my robots to trespass? Set fire to your orchards? What will provoke you, Holt?"

"Nothing," Holt said. "I don't want to kill you. Get someone else to do it."

The eyes glittered. "You devil," McDermott said. "You absolute devil. I never realized how much you hated me. I send for you in a time of need, asking to be put out of my misery, and will you grant me that? Oh, no. Suddenly you get noble. You won't kill me! You devil, I see right through you. You'll go back to your keep and gloat because I'm a living dead man here. You'll chuckle to yourself because I'm alone and frozen into this capsule. Oh, Holt, it's not right to hate so deeply! I admit I've given offense. I deliberately built the tower here to wound your pride. Punish me, then. Take my life. Destroy my tower. Don't leave me here!"

Holt was silent. He moistened his lips, filled his lungs with breath, got to his feet. He stood straight and tall, towering over the capsule that held his enemy.

"Throw the switch," McDermott begged.

"I'm sorry. I can't."

"Devil!"

Holt looked at his robots. "It's time to go," he said. "There's no need for you to guide us. We can find our way out of the building."

The teardrop-shaped car sped across the shining snow. Holt said nothing as he made the return journey. His mind clung to the image of the immobilized McDermott, and there was no room for any other thought. That stench of decay tingled in his nostrils. That glint of madness in the eyes as they begged for oblivion.

They were crossing the borderlands, now. Holt's car broke the warning barrier and got a pinging signal to halt and identify. A robot gave the password, and they went on toward Holt Keep.

His family clustered near the entrance, pale, mystified. Holt walked in under his own steam. They were bursting with questions, but no one dared ask anything. It remained for Holt to say the first word.

He said, "McDermott's a sick, crazy old man. His family is dead or gone. He's a pathetic and disgusting sight. I don't want to talk about the visit."

Sweeping past them, Holt ascended the shaft to the command room. He peered out, over the snowy field. There was a double track in the snow, leading to and from McDermott Keep, and the sunlight blazed in the track, making it a line of fire stretching to the horizon.

The building shuddered suddenly. Holt heard a hiss and a whine. He flipped on his communicator and a robot voice said, "McDermott Keep is attacking, your lordship. We've deflected a high-energy bombardment."

"Did the screens have any trouble with it?"

"No, your lordship. Not at all. Shall I prepare for a counterattack?"

Holt smiled. "No," he said. "Take defensive measures only. Extend the screens right to the border and keep them there. Don't let McDermott do any harm. He's only trying to provoke me, but he won't succeed."

The tall, gaunt man walked to the control panel. His gnarled hands rested lovingly on the equipment. So they had come to warfare at last, he thought. The cannon of McDermott Keep were doing their puny worst. Flickering needles told the story: whatever McDermott was throwing was being absorbed easily. He didn't have the firepower to do real harm.

Holt's hands tightened on the controls. Now, he thought, he could blast McDermott Keep to ash. But he would not do it, any more than he would throw the switch that would end Andrew McDermott's life.

McDermott did not understand. Not cruelty, but simple selfishness, had kept him from killing the enemy lord, just as, all these years, Holt had refrained from launching an attack he was certain to win. He felt remotely sorry for the paralyzed man locked in the life-capsule. But it was inconceivable that Holt would kill him.

Once you are gone, Andrew, whom will I have to hate? Holt wondered.

That was why he had not killed. No reason more complicated than that.

Michael Holt peered through the foot-thick safety glass of his command-room window. He saw the zone of brown earth, the snowfield with its fresh track, and the coppery ugliness of McDermott Keep. His intestines writhed at the ugliness of that baroque tower against the horizon. He imagined the skyline as it had looked a hundred years ago, before McDermott had built his foul monstrosity there.

He fondled the controls of his artillery bank as though they were a young girl's breasts. Then he turned, slowly and stiffly, making his way across the command room to his chair, and sat quietly, listening to the sound of Andrew McDermott's futile bombardment expending itself harmlessly against the outer defenses of Holt Keep, and soon it grew dark as the winter night closed quietly down.

Passport to Sirius

Consumer Sixth Class David Carman watched the yellow snake that was the morning telefax sheet come rippling from the wall slot of his bachelor flat. The folds of plastic-impregnated tape slithered into the receiving tray, and Carman surveyed them glumly. He knew there would only be more bad news—more tales of defeat in the Sirian war, more heralding of price increases on the consumer front.

After a moment of hesitation Carman gathered up the telefax spool and slipped it into the scanner-reader. He shuddered as the first news appeared on the screen.

COSTLY SETBACK IN SIRIUS

War Sector, 14 Nov (via subradio)—A Sirian pitchfork maneuver hurled Earth lines back today in the battle for Sirius IV. The sudden alien thrust cost Earth eight destroyers and more than a hundred casualties.

The push began, according to a front-lines communique, when eleven Sirian battle cruisers initiated diversionary tactics in orbit around the Earth base on Sirius IV's seventh moon. Bringing in a battalion of mosquito ships next, the aliens successfully—

Morosely Carman thumbed his weary eyes and moved the scanner further along. All these war stories were pretty much alike, he thought. And the telefax reveled in detailed descriptions of each offensive and defensive tactic. Carman knew nothing of war-making; the details bored him.

But the next item was hardly more cheering.

PRICE INDEX TO JUMP AGAIN

Lower Urb-district, 16 Nov—Consumer prices are due for another increase spiral as a result of the severe setback suffered by Terran forces in the Sirian sector. Economic Regulator Harrison Morch revealed this morning that a down-the-line 5% increase is likely.

"We tried to hold the line," commented Regulator Morch. "The inflationary trend was too strong to buck, however. It is to be hoped that conclusion of hostilities will soon bring about a reversion to peacetime living standards and—"

With an angry, impatient gesture, Carman blanked the screen. There was little sense spending good money subscribing to the 'fax service if it only brought bad news.

Things hadn't been this bad a year ago, before the war started, he thought, as he dialed breakfast and took his seat by the dispensall. He had even been thinking of applying for a marriage permit, then. Now, of course, it was out of the question; his economic status was totally altered. And Sally, who worked for the Bureau of Extraterrestrial Affairs, had received a pay boost that put her entirely beyond Carman's aspirations. She was Third Class, now, and would soon marry a wealthy bureau official.

Carman broodingly munched his somewhat dry algae omelet. He was thirty-three, and not getting younger. He was too pale, too thin, his eyes too close-set, his hair growing sparse. And it seemed that whenever he got some money saved and looked around to better his position, along came some war to send prices shooting up and cripple his savings. Five years ago there had been that thing in Procyon, and then a year or two of peace followed by a scuffle out near Proxima Centauri. And now Sirius.

You can't win, he thought. He finished breakfast mechanically, dropped the dishes in the disposall, and selected his second-best suit with a quick, bitter jab at the wardrobe control buttons.

It came issuing forth: gray crepe, with dark-blue trim. The jacket was getting tattered at the elbows.

I'd better buy a new suit, Carman decided, as he stepped out on the pickup platform to hail a jet-cab. *Before clothing prices get astronomical.*

He reached the office at 0700 that morning, with dawn barely brightening the late autumn sky. Carman worked as a sorter in the permit-processing department of the Confederation Passport Office, and so as a government employee had little recourse when the periodic inflation spirals came; he could hardly go on strike against the Confederation.

A good-sized batch of passport applications had already accumulated at his receiving tray. Carman slid easily into the seat, flashed bright but hollow smiles at the five or six fellow workers nearest him, and grabbed at the top sheet of the stack. He estimated quickly that 180 applications had arrived so far. They would be pouring in at a rate of seven a minute the rest of the day.

He computed:

If I process one form every six seconds, ten a minute, I'll gain three per minute on them. Which means I'll catch up with them in about an hour.

If he kept up the ten-a-minute pace, he'd be free to take short breathers later on. This was one of the games he played to make his dreary work more palatable.

The first application was from Consumer Second Class Leebig D. Quellen and family; Consumer Second Class Quellen wanted to visit the Ganymede outpost next summer. Carman plunged the application into the bin stencil-labelled *14a* with his left hand, and with his right took another from the waiting stack. Sort with the left, grab with the right. Carman swayed rhythmically in his seat as he fell into the pattern of the day's work.

After a while he began hitting them twelve to a minute, sometimes thirteen. By 0757 his tray was empty. He sighed. Eight seconds of free time, now, until the next permit reared its ugly head.

Sort, grab . . . sort, grab . . . it was dull but essentially simple work, in a mechanical way. It scarcely taxed his brain. But he was paid accordingly: $163 a week, barely a subsistence wage before the last spiral. And now—

Soon 1030 came. Break time. Carman stretched and rose, noticing angrily that the girl in the upstairs receiving room had slipped three applications in after break time sounded. She was always pulling tricks like that.

Carman had long since reduced break time to a ritual. He crossed the office to the cleanall and held his hands in the energizing bath until his fingertips were wiped clean of their accumulation of stylus grime; then he glanced out the single big window at the crowded city, turned, and smiled at Montano, the heavy-set fellow who had occupied the next desk for the six years Carman had worked for the Passport Office.

"Nice day," Montano said. "For November."

"Yes."

"See the morning 'fax? Looks like another upping for prices."

Carman nodded unhappily. "I saw. Don't know how we'll manage."

"Oh, we'll get along. We always do. The wife's due for a raise soon anyway." Montano's wife pushed buttons in a car autofactory. Somehow she seemed to be due for a raise almost every other week.

"That's nice," Carman said.

"Yeah."

"Does she think cars are going up?"

"Damn right," Montano said. "Ford-Chrysler's boosting the stock model to six thousand next month. Need turbogenerators for the war effort, they say. We already got our order in at the old price. You better buy fast if you want one, Carman. Save five hundred bucks now if you're smart."

"I don't need a new car," Carman said.

"Better get *anything* you need now, anyway. Everything's going up. Always does, wartime."

The bell tone announced the end of break time. Carman reached his desk just in time to see a passport application come fluttering down, followed seconds later by another.

"Demons take that girl," he muttered softly. She always cut her break short to plague him with extra work. Now she was six—no, seven—ahead of him.

Justin C. Froelich and family, of Minnetonka, wished permission to visit Pluto next July. Wearily, Carman dropped Justin C. Froelich's application in the proper bin, and reached for the next.

He was seething inwardly, cursing the Passport Office, the girl upstairs, inflation, Economic Regulator Morch, and the world in general. It seemed to be a rat race with no exit from the treadmill.

I've been pushed around too long, he thought. *I ought to fight back a little. Somehow.*

Consumer Sixth Class Carman was on the verge of changing the course of his life. An hour more passed, and 193 additional passport applications disappeared into bins. Finally, he made up his mind to act.

The recruiting officer was a spade-faced, dark-complexioned man with angular features and bright white teeth. He wore the green-and-gold uniform of the United Military Services of Earth. He stared levelly across his shining bare desk at Carman and said, "Would you mind repeating that?"

"I said I wanted to fight. Against Sirius."

The recruiting officer frowned ponderously. After a long pause he said, "I don't see how I can guarantee that. We enroll you; the computer ships you out. Whether you get sent to the war zone or not depends on a variable complex of factors which certainly no civilian should be expected to understand." He shoved a form across the desk toward Carman. "If you'll fill this out, Mac, we can—"

"No," Carman said. "I want a guarantee that I'll see action in the Sirius sector. Dammit, Lieutenant—"

"Sergeant."

"—Sergeant, I'm thirty-three. I'm as close to being nobody as anybody can get. If I'm lucky I'll get as high as Third Class someday. I've saved ten thousand bucks, and I suppose the new inflation's going to knock my savings in half the way the last one did."

"Mr. Carman, I don't see how all this—"

"You will. For thirty-three years I've been sitting around on the home front going up and down with each economic spiral while Earth fights wars in Procyon and Proxima C and half a dozen other places. I'm tired of staying home. I want to enlist."

"Sure, Mac, but—"

"But I don't want to enlist just to wear a uniform and police the frontiers on Betelgeuse. I want to go to Sirius, and I want to fight. Once in my life I want to engage in positive action on behalf of a Cause." Carman took a deep breath; he hadn't spoken this many words in succession in a long, long time. "Do you understand now? Will you guarantee that I'll be shipped to Sirius if I sign up?"

The sergeant exhaled deeply, unhappily. "I've explained twice that the matter's not in my hands. Maybe I could attach a recommendation—"

"A *guarantee*."

"But—" A crafty light appeared in the recruiting sergeant's eyes; he drummed the desk top momentarily and said, "You're a very persistent man, Mac. You win; I'll see you get assigned to the war zone. Now, why don't you just sign your name here—"

Carman shook his head. "No, thanks. I just changed my mind."

Before the sergeant could protest, Carman had backed warily out of the office and was gone. It had abruptly occurred to him that a recruiting officer's promise was not necessarily final. And there were more direct methods he could use to get into the war.

He returned to the Passport Office at 1313, and the robot eye at the office door took note of it, clicking loudly as he passed through. Ordinarily Carman would have groaned at the loss of thirteen minutes' pay, but, then, ordinarily he would have been at his desk promptly at 1300 anyway.

Everyone else was busily at work; heads bowed, hands groping madly for the incoming applications, his fellow sorters presented an oddly ludicrous sight. Carman resumed his place. Nearly a hundred waiting permits had stacked themselves in the receiving tray during his absence—but this, too, hardly troubled him now.

He went through them at a frantic pace, occasionally hitting as high as twenty per minute. Plenty of them were going to the wrong bins, he realized, but this was no time to worry about that. He caught up with the posting department in less than forty minutes, and made use of his first eight-second breather to draw a blank passport application from his desk drawer; he had always kept a few on hand there.

He filled out the blank patiently, in eight-second bursts between each of the arrivals from above. Where it said

Name and Status, he wrote *Consumer Sixth Class David Carman.* Where it said *Intended Destination,* he inscribed *Sirius VII* in tidy cursives. Sirius VII was outside the war zone, and so theoretically within reach of commercial traffic, but passports to anywhere in the Sirius system were granted only by special dispensation since the outbreak of hostilities, and Carman knew he had small chance of receiving such dispensation.

Which was why, after the form was completely filled out, he thoughtfully scribbled an expert forgery of the Secretary of Extraterrestrial Affairs' signature on the bottom of the sheet, okaying the application. Humming gently, he dropped the completed blank into the bin labeled *82g* and returned his attention to the labors of the day.

The passport took eight days to come through. Carman had some uneasy moments while waiting, though he was ultimately confident of success. After all, the workers who processed the sorted applications and issued the passports probably handled their work as mechanically and hastily as he did in the level above them—and he never had time to check for possible forgeries, so why should they? Never-ending cascades of passport applications descended on them; probably they cursed him for working so fast, just as he in turn scowled up the chute at the girl in the top level.

Five seconds after the passport to Sirius dropped out of his mail chute, Carman was on the phone talking to the secretary of the Personnel Chief at the Passport Office.

"Yes, I said Carman. David Carman, Sixth Class. I've enlisted in the Services and my resignation is effective today. Yes, *today.* My pay check? Oh, burn it," Carman said impatiently, and hung up. So much for past associations.

Carman withdrew his entire savings—$9,783.61. The roboteller handed over the cash without comment. Carman took the thick pile of crisp bills, counted slowly through them to the great annoyance of the people behind him in line, and nudged the *acknowledge* stud to let the teller know the transaction was complete. Outside the bank, he signaled for another copter and took it to the Upper Urbdistrict Spaceport, far out on what had once been Long Island.

"A ticket to Sirius?" the dispatcher asked, after the robot ticket vender had passed Carman on to him in perplexity. "But the war, you know—we've curtailed our service to that entire sector."

"I don't care," Carman said stolidly. He was growing accustomed to being forceful now; it came easily to him, and he enjoyed it. "You advertise through transportation to Sirius VII. I've got a passport that says I can go there, and I've got six thousand dollars to pay my way. Cash."

"This is very irregular," moaned the dispatcher, a short, harried-looking little man. "We discontinued passenger service to that system eight months ago, when—"

"You could lose your franchise for this," Carman snapped bluntly. "Sirius VII is nonbelligerent. I have money and a passport. I demand transportation."

In the end, they diverted a freight run bound for Deneb, and put Carman aboard with the promise that they'd drop him at Sirius VII. His passport was in order, and he had the cash for the payment.

The trip took three weeks of steady hyperdrive travel. Six other humans were on board, all bad-smelling crewmen, and the crew of a space freighter is hardly pleasant company on a three-week journey. Carman kept to himself, inventing a form of solitaire he could play making use of hundred-dollar bills, of which he had more than thirty left even after paying passage. The ship's cargo consisted of steers slated for an agrarian colony orbiting Deneb, and Carman lived in a cramped cabin just aft of the cargo hold. He got little sleep.

They put him down finally on the concrete landing apron at Zuorf, crown city of Sirius VII, on the fifth day of 2672, having first radioed the Terran consul there to let them know he was coming. Biggest and muggiest of the twelve planets that circled the dog star, Sirius VII was a vast mountainous world with ugly sprawling cities crammed between the jagged peaks; its people were brawny ursinoids, not long escaped from their neolithic culture stage.

As it happened, some sort of local celebration was in full sway when Carman, a solitary figure with a solitary suitcase of belongings, left the spaceport. Great heavy-set creatures were whirling up and down the streets in each other's arms, looking like so many dancing bears clad in tinsel and frills. Carman stepped hastily back into the shadow of a squat yellow-painted building while a platoon of the huge shaggy aliens came thundering past, to the gay accompaniment of distant tootling music composed in excruciating quarter-tone intervals.

A hand fell lightly on his shoulder. Carman turned and jumped away all in the same nervous motion. He saw an Earthman behind him, clad in the somber black vestments of the Terran diplomatic corps.

"Pardon me if I startled you," the stranger said in a soft, cultured voice. He was a neatly turned out, mildly foppish-looking man in his forties, with elegant features, well-groomed dark hair, delicately shaven brow ridges. Only the startling brass ring through his nostrils marred his otherwise distinguished upper-class appearance.

"I'm the Terran consul on this world," he went on, in

the same gentle tones. "Adrian Blyde's my name. Am I right in assuming you're the man who was just dropped off by that freighter?"

"You are. I'm David Carman of Earth. Want to see my passport?"

Consul Blyde smiled serenely. "In due time, Mr. Carman. I'm sure it's in good order. But would you mind telling me precisely *why* you've come to Sirius VII?"

"To join the armed forces. I want to take part in the Sirian campaign."

"To join the armed forces," Blyde repeated in a faintly wonder-struck voice. "Well, well, well. That's very interesting, Mr. Carman. Very. Would you come this way, please?"

Blyde seized him firmly by the fleshy part of his arm and propelled him across the wide, poorly paved street, between two pairs of madly careening bearlike beings, and into a narrow doorway in a building constructed of purple brick.

"The autochthones are celebrating their annual fertility dance through the city from morning to night without rest. Those that keep on their feet the whole day without collapsing are entitled to mate. The weak ones have to try again next year. It's quite a neat genetic system, really."

Carman glanced back through the doorway at the hordes of spinning aliens weaving wildly down the broad street, locked each to each in a desperate grip of love.

"The nose rings denote masculinity," Blyde said. "Terran males who stay here have to wear them too; the natives are very, very fussy about that. When in Rome, you know. I'll give you yours tonight."

"Just a minute," Carman said worriedly, as Blyde unlocked an office door and gestured within to a cluttered little room lined with book tapes and scattered papers. "I don't plan to stay here, you know. The military action's on Sirius IV. That's where I'm going as soon as I've seen the authorities and enlisted."

Blyde dropped heavily into a well-upholstered pneumo-chair, wiped perspiration from his brow with an obviously scented cloth, and sighed unhappily. "My dear Mr. Carman: I don't know what motives impelled you to come to this system, nor by what chicanery you wangled your passage. But now that you're here, there are several things you should know."

"Such as?"

"For one, there are no hostilities currently taking place anywhere in the Sirius system."

Stunned, Carman gasped, "No—hostilities? Then the war's over?"

Blyde touched his fingertips lightly together. "You misunderstand. There never *was* any war between Earth and Sirius IV. Care for a drink?"

"Rye," Carman said automatically. "Never—was—a—war? But—how—"

"Economic Regulator Harrison Morch of Earth is a great man," Blyde said with seeming irrelevancy, putting his head back as if studying the reticulated pattern of paint cracks on the office ceiling. An air-conditioner hummed ineffectually somewhere. "Economic Regulator Morch has devoted a lifetime of study to examining the motives governing fluctuations in economic trends."

Carman's throat felt terribly dry. The moist warmth of Sirius VII's atmosphere, the additional drag of the heavier gravity, the calm blandness of the consul's manner, the sheer nonsense he was talking—all these factors were combining to make Carman thoroughly sick.

"What does all this have to do with—"

Blyde raised one manicured hand. "Economic Regulator Morch, through his studies, has reduced to a formula the general economic principle known to theorists for centuries—that spending increases in direct proportion to adverse military news. Consumers go on buying sprees, remembering the last cycle of shortages and of rapid price increases. Money flows more freely. Of course, when the war situation lasts long enough, a period of inflation sets in—making it necessary that an equally virulent peace be waged."

Dimly Carman sensed what was coming. "No," he said.

"Yes. There is no war with Sirius. It was a stroke of genius on Economic Regulator Morch's part to take advantage of the uncertainty of interstellar communication to enforce a news block on the entire Sirius system. It's a simple matter to distribute fabricated war communiqués, invent wholly fictitious spaceships which perish gorily on the demand of the moment, arouse public interest and keep it at a high pitch—"

"You mean," Carman said tonelessly, "that Morch invented this whole war, and arranges Terran victories and losses to fit economic conditions back home?"

"It is a brilliant plan," said Blyde, smiling complacently. "If a decline in spending occurs, word of severe losses in space reaches the home front, and the bad news serves to unloose the purse strings. When the economy has been reinflated, Earth's legions forge on to victory, and spending drops off again. We spend heavily in times of stress, when we need consolation—not in peacetime."

Carman blinked. "I spent six thousand dollars and forged a passport to come here and find out *this!* The one time in my life I decided to *do* something, instead of sitting back and letting things happen to me, I discover it's all a hoax." He flexed his fingers experimentally, as if wondering what he might do with them.

Blyde seemed to be sympathetic. "It is, I realize, terribly awkward for you. But no more so than it is to us, who have the strenuous task of preserving this beneficial hoax and protecting it from would-be exposers."

"Are you going to kill me, then?"

Blyde blanched at the blunt question. "Mr. Carman! We are not barbarians!"

"Well, what *are* you going to do with me?"

The consul shrugged. "The one completely satisfactory thing. We'll find you a good job here on Sirius VII. You'll be much happier here than you ever were on Earth. Naturally, you can't be permitted to return home."

But the man who can forge a passport to Sirius can also find a way home. In Carman's case it took him seven full months—months of living in the sticky, endless heat of Sirius VII, dodging the playful ursinoid natives, kowtowing to Blyde (whose secretary he became, at $60 a week) and wearing a brass nose ring through his nostrils.

It was seven months before he had mastered Blyde's signature to his own satisfaction, and knew enough of local diplomatic protocol to be able to requisition a spaceship from the small military outpost just outside Zuorf. A messenger—there were no phones on the planet, for obscure religious reasons—came to the Consulate to announce that the ship was ready.

"Wait outside," Carman told the boy.

Blyde looked up from behind his desk and said, "What ship does he mean?"

"The one I'm taking back to Earth," said Carman, and released the sleep capsule. Blyde smiled sweetly as he slipped into unconsciousness. Carman followed the boy to the spaceport.

A slim, trim two-man ship waited there, sleek and golden-hulled in the bright sunlight. The pilot was an efficient-looking space-tanned man named Duane.

"Diplomatic pouch," Carman said, handing over the leather attaché case he had prepared for the occasion. Duane stored it reverently in the hold, and they blasted off.

"Sirius IV first," Carman ordered. "I'm supposed to take films. Top secret, of course."

"Of course."

They circled the small pockmarked gray fourth planet at fifty-thousand feet, and Carman took enough cloud-piercing infrared shots to prove conclusively that there was not and never had been any war between the amiable amphibious aborigines and Earth. Satisfied, he ordered the pilot to proceed immediately toward Sol.

They reached Earth nineteen days later, on August 3, 2672. A squad of security police was waiting for them as they landed at Upper Urbdistrict Spaceport, and Carman was swiftly conveyed to a cell in Confederation Detention House in the tunnels far below Old Manhattan. Blyde had sent word ahead via subradio concerning Carman's escape, it seemed.

In his cell, later that evening, Carman was visited by a parched-looking, almost fleshless man in the blue cape and red wig of high governmental office.

"So you're the culprit!"

"That's what they tell me. Who are you?"

"Ferdan Veller, Administrative Assistant to Regulator Morch. The Regulator sent me to see who you were and what you were like."

"Well, now you've seen," Carman said. "Get out."

Assistant Veller's melancholy eyes widened. "I see you're a forceful man, Mr. Carman. No doubt you're full of plans for escaping, recapturing your confiscated films, and letting the world know what a dastardly hoax is being perpetrated in the interests of a balanced economy. Eh?"

"I might be," Carman admitted.

"You might be interested in this morning's telefax sheet, then," Veller said. He extended a torn-off yellow strip.

The headline was:

NEW AGGRESSION
THREATENS EARTH!

Government City, 3 Aug 2672—Word reached Earth today of yet another threat to her peace, coming hot on the heels of the recently concluded police action in the Sirius sector. Forces in the Great Andromeda Nebula have issued statements inimical to Earth, and a new conflict looms—"

"You killed off Sirius because you were afraid I'd expose it," Carman said accusingly. "And now you're starting up a new one."

Veller nodded smugly. "Quite. The Great Andromeda Nebula happens to be nine hundred thousand light-years away. The round trip, even by hyperdrive, takes some twenty years." He grinned, showing a double row of square, tartared teeth. "You're a forceful man, Mr. Carman. You may very well escape. You may even reach Andromeda and return with evidence once again unmasking us. If you live long enough to return, that is. I think our economic program is in no immediate danger from you."

He left, smiling gravely. The cell door closed with a harsh metallic crash.

"Come back!" Carman yelled. "You can't hoax mankind like that! I'll let everyone know! I'll get out and expose—"

There was no answer, not even a catcall. No one was listening. And, Carman realized dully, no one was going to listen to him at all, ever again.

Caught in the Organ Draft

Look there, Kate, down by the promenade. Two splendid seniors walking side by side near the water's edge. They radiate power, authority, wealth, assurance. He's a judge, a senator, a corporation president, no doubt, and she's—what?—a professor emeritus of international law, let's say. There they go toward the plaza, moving serenely, smiling, nodding graciously to passersby. How the sunlight gleams in their white hair! I can barely stand the brilliance of that reflected aura: it blinds me, it stings my eyes. What are they, eighty, ninety, a hundred years old? At this distance they seem much younger—they hold themselves upright, their backs are straight, they might pass for being only fifty or sixty. But I can tell. Their confidence, their poise, mark them for what they are. And when they were nearer I could see their withered cheeks, their sunken eyes. No cosmetics can hide that. These two are old enough to be our great-grandparents. They were well past sixty before we were even born, Kate. How superbly their bodies function! But why not? We can guess at their medical histories. She's had at least three hearts, he's working on his fourth set of lungs, they apply for new kidneys every five years, their brittle bones are reinforced with hundreds of skeletal snips from the arms and legs of hapless younger folk, their dimming sensory apparatus is aided by countless nerve grafts obtained the same way, their ancient arteries are freshly sheathed with sleek teflon. Ambulatory assemblages of second-hand human parts, spiced here and there with synthetic or mechanical organ-substitutes, that's all they are. And what am I, then, or you? Nineteen years old and vulnerable. In their eyes I'm nothing but a ready stockpile of healthy organs, waiting to serve their needs. Come here, son. What a fine strapping young man you are! Can you spare a kidney for me? A lung? A choice little segment of intestine? Ten centimeters of your ulnar nerve? I need a few pieces of you, lad. You won't deny a distinguished elder leader like me what I ask, will you? *Will you?*

Today my draft notice, a small crisp document, very official-looking, came shooting out of the data slot when I punched for my morning mail. I've been expecting it all spring: no surprise, no shock, actually rather an anti-climax now that it's finally here. In six weeks I am to report to Transplant House for my final physical exam—only a formality. They wouldn't have drafted me if I didn't already rate top marks as organ-reservoir potential—and then I go on call. The average call time is about two months. By autumn they'll be carving me up. Eat, drink, and be merry, for soon comes the surgeon to my door.

A straggly band of senior citizens is picketing the central headquarters of the League for Bodily Sanctity. It's a counterdemonstration, an anti-anti-transplant protest, the worst kind of political statement, feeding on the ugliest of negative emotions. The demonstrators carry glowing signs that say:

> BODILY SANCTITY—OR
> BODILY SELFISHNESS?

and:

YOU OWE YOUR
LEADERS YOUR
VERY LIVES

and:

LISTEN TO THE VOICE
OF EXPERIENCE

The picketers are low-echelon seniors, barely across the qualifying line, the ones who can't really be sure of getting transplants. No wonder they're edgy about the League. Some of them are in wheelchairs and some are encased right up to the eyebrows in portable life-support systems. They croak and shout bitter invective and shake their fists. Watching the show from an upper window of the League building, I shiver with fear and dismay. These people don't just want my kidneys or my lungs. They'd take my eyes, my liver, my pancreas, my heart, anything they might happen to need.

I talked it over with my father. He's forty-five years old—too old to have been personally affected by the organ draft, too young to have needed any transplants yet. That puts him in a neutral position, so to speak, except for one minor factor: his transplant status is 5-G. That's quite high on the eligibility list, not the top-priority class but close enough. If he fell ill tomorrow and the Transplant Board ruled that his life would be endangered if he didn't get a new heart or lung or kidney, he'd be given one practically immediately. Status like that simply has to influence his objectivity on the whole organ issue. Anyway, I told him I was planning to appeal and maybe even to resist. "Be reasonable," he said, "be rational, don't let your emotions run away with you. Is it worth jeopardizing your whole future over a thing like this? After all, not everybody who's drafted loses vital organs."

"Show me the statistics," I said. "Show me."

He didn't know the statistics. It was his impression that only about a quarter or a fifth of the draftees actually got an organ call. That tells you how closely the older generation keeps in touch with the situation—and my father's an educated man, articulate, well informed. Nobody over the age of thirty-five that I talked to could show me any statistics. So I showed them. Out of a League brochure, it's true, but based on certified National Institute of Health reports. Nobody escapes. They always clip you, once you qualify. The need for young organs inexorably expands to match the pool of available organ-power. In the long run they'll get us all and chop us to bits. That's probably what they want, anyway. To rid themselves of the younger members of the species, always so troublesome, by cannibalizing us for spare parts, and recycling us, lung by lung, pancreas by pancreas, through their own deteriorating bodies.

On March 23, 1964, this dog's own liver was removed and replaced with the liver of a non-related mongrel donor. The animal was treated with azathioprine for 4 months and all therapy then stopped. He remains in perfect health 6⅔ years after transplantation.

The war goes on. This is, I think, its fourteenth year. Of course they're beyond the business of killing now. They haven't had any field engagements since '93 or so, certainly none since the organ-draft legislation went into effect. The old ones can't afford to waste precious young bodies on the battlefield. So robots wage our territorial struggles for us, butting heads with a great metallic clank, laying mines and twitching their sensors at the enemy's mines, digging tunnels beneath his screens, et cetera, et cetera. Plus, of course, the quasi-military activity—economic sanctions, third-power blockades, propaganda telecasts beamed as overrides from merciless orbital satellites, and stuff like that. It's a subtler war than the kind they used to wage: nobody dies. Still, it drains national resources. Taxes are going up again this year, the fifth or sixth year in a row, and they've just slapped a special Peace Surcharge on all metal-containing goods, on account of the copper shortage. There once was a time when we could hope that our crazy old leaders would die off or at least retire for reasons of health, stumbling away to their country villas with ulcers or shingles or scabies or scruples and allowing new young peace-makers to take office. But now they just go on and on, immortal and insane, our senators, our cabinet members, our generals, our planners. And their war goes on and on too, their absurd, incomprehensible, diabolical, self-gratifying war.

I know people my age or a little older who have taken asylum in Belgium or Sweden or Paraguay or one of the other countries where Bodily Sanctity laws have been passed. There are about twenty such countries, half of them the most progressive nations in the world and half of them the most reactionary. But what's the sense of running away? I don't want to live in exile. I'll stay here and fight.

Naturally they don't ask a draftee to give up his heart or his liver or some other organ essential to life, say his medulla oblongata. We haven't yet reached that stage of political enlightenment at which the government feels capable of legislating fatal conscription. Kidneys and lungs, the paired organs, the dispensable organs, are the chief targets so far. But if you study the history of conscription over the ages you see that it can always be projected on a curve rising from rational necessity to absolute lunacy. Give them a fingertip, they'll take an arm. Give them an inch of bowel, they'll take your guts. In another fifty years they'll be drafting hearts and stomachs and maybe even brains, mark my words; let them get the technology of brain transplants together and nobody's skull will be safe. It'll be human sacrifice all over again. The only difference between us and the Aztecs is one of method: we have anesthesia, we have antisepsis and asepsis, we use scalpels instead of obsidian blades to cut out the hearts of our victims.

MEANS OF OVERCOMING
THE HOMOGRAFT
REACTION

The pathway that has led from the demonstration of the immunological nature of the homograft reaction and its universality to the development of relatively effective but by no means completely satisfactory means of overcoming it for therapeutic purposes is an interesting one that can only be touched upon very briefly. The year 1950 ushered in a new era in transplantation immunobiology in which the discovery of various means of weakening or abrogating a host's response to a homograft—such as sublethal whole body X-irradiation, or treatment with certain adrenal corticosteroid hormones, notably cortisone—began to influence the direction of the mainstream of research and engender confidence that a workable clinical solution might not be too far off. By the end of the decade, powerful immuno-suppressive drugs, such as 6-mercaptopurine, had been shown to be capable of holding in abeyance the reactivity of dogs to renal homografts, and soon afterwards this principle was successfully extended to man.

Is my resistance to the draft based on an ingrained abstract distaste for tyranny in all forms, or rather on the mere desire to keep my body intact? Could it be both, maybe? Do I need an idealistic rationalization at all? Don't I have an inalienable right to go through my life wearing my own native-born kidneys?

The law was put through by an administration of old men. You can be sure that all laws affecting the welfare of the young are the work of doddering moribund ancients afflicted with angina pectoris, atherosclerosis, prolapses of the infundibulum, fulminating ventricles, and dilated viaducts. The problem was this: not enough healthy young people were dying of highway accidents, successful suicide attempts, diving-board miscalculations, electrocutions, and football injuries; therefore there was a shortage of transplantable organs. An effort to restore the death penalty for the sake of creating a steady supply of state-controlled cadavers lost out in the courts. Volunteer programs of organ donation weren't working out too well, since most of the volunteers were criminals who signed up in order to gain early release from prison: a lung reduced your sentence by five years, a kidney got you three years off, and so on. The exodus of convicts from the jails under this clause wasn't so popular among suburban voters. Meanwhile there was an urgent and mounting need for organs; a lot of important seniors might in fact die if something didn't get done fast. So a coalition of senators from all four parties rammed the organ-draft measure through the upper chamber in the face of a filibuster threat from a few youth-oriented members. It had a much easier time in the House of Representatives, since nobody in the House ever pays much attention to the text of a bill up for a vote, and word had been circulated on this one that if it passed, everybody over sixty-five who had any political pull at all could count on living twenty or thirty extra years, which to a representative means a crack at ten to fifteen extra terms of office. Naturally there have been court challenges, but what's the use? The average age of the eleven justices of the Supreme Court is seventy-eight. They're human and mortal. They need our flesh. If they throw out the organ draft now, they are signing their own death warrants.

For a year and a half I was the chairman of the anti-draft campaign on our campus. We were the sixth or seventh local chapter of the League for Bodily Sanctity to be organized in this country, and we were real activists. Mainly we would march up and down in front of the draft board offices carrying signs proclaiming things like:

KIDNEY POWER

and:

A MAN'S BODY IS
HIS CASTLE

and:

THE POWER TO
CONSCRIPT ORGANS
IS THE POWER TO
DESTROY LIVES

We never went in for the rough stuff, though, like bombing organ-transplant centers or hijacking refrigeration trucks. Peaceful agitation, that was our motto. When a couple of our members tried to swing us to a more violent policy, I delivered an extemporaneous two-hour speech arguing for moderation. Naturally, I was drafted the moment I became eligible.

"I can understand your hostility to the draft," my college adviser said. "It's certainly normal to feel queasy about surrendering important organs of your body. But you ought to consider the countervailing advantages. Once you've given an organ you get a 6-A classification, Preferred Recipient, and you remain forever on the 6-A roster. Surely you realize that this means that if you ever need a transplant yourself, you'll automatically be eligible for one, even if your other personal and professional qualifications don't lift you to the optimum level. Suppose your career plans don't work out and you become a manual laborer, for instance. Ordinarily you wouldn't rate even a first look if you developed heart disease, but your Preferred Recipient status would save you. You'd get a new lease on life, my boy."

I pointed out the fallacy inherent in this. Which is that as the number of draftees increases, it will come to encompass a majority or even a totality of the population, and eventually everybody will have 6-A Preferred Recipient status by virtue of having donated, and the term Preferred Recipient will cease to have any meaning. A shortage of transplantable organs would eventually develop as each past donor stakes his claim to a transplant when his health fails, and in time they'd have to arrange the Preferred Recipients by order of personal and professional achievement anyway, for the sake of arriving at some kind of priorities within the 6-A class, and we'd be right back where we are now.

The course of a patient who received antilymphocyte globulin (ALG) before and for the first 4 months after renal homotransplantation. The donor was an older brother. There was no early rejection. Prednisone therapy was started 40 days postoperatively. Note the insidious onset of late rejection after cessation of globulin therapy. This was treated by a moderate increase in the maintenance doses of steroids. This delayed complication occurred in only 2 of the first 20 recipients of intrafamilial homografts who were treated with ALG. It has been seen with about the same low frequency in subsequent cases. (By permission of Surg. Gynec. Obstet. 126 (1968): p. 1023.)

So I went down to Transplant House today, right on schedule, to take my physical. A couple of my friends thought I was making a tactical mistake by reporting at all; if you're going to resist, they said, resist at every point along the line. Make them drag you in for the physical. In purely idealistic (and ideological) terms, I suppose they're right. But there's no need yet for me to start kicking up a fuss. Wait till they actually say, "We need your kidney, young man." Then I can resist, if resistance is the course I ultimately choose. (Why am I wavering? Am I not entirely convinced of the injustice of the entire organ-draft system? I don't know. I'm not even sure that I *am* wavering. Reporting for your physical isn't really a sellout to the system.) I went, anyway. They tapped this and X-rayed that and peered into the other thing. Yawn, please. Bend over, please. Cough, please. Hold out your left arm, please. They marched me in front of a battery of diagnostat machines and I stood there hoping for the red light to flash—*tilt, get out of here!*— but I was, as expected, in perfect physical shape, and I qualified for call. Afterward, I met Kate and we walked in the park and held hands and watched the glories of the sunset and discussed what I'll do, when and if the call comes. *If?* Wishful thinking, boy!

If your number is called you become exempt from military service, and they credit you with a special $750 tax deduction every year. Big deal.

Another thing they're very proud of is the program of voluntary donation of unpaired organs. This has nothing to do with the draft, which—this far, at least—requisitions only paired organs, organs that can be spared without loss of life. For the last twelve years it's been possible to walk into any hospital in the United States and sign a simple release form allowing the surgeons to slice you up. Eyes, lungs, heart, intestines, pancreas, liver—anything, you give it all to them. This process used to be known as suicide in a simpler era and it was socially disapproved, especially in times of labor shortages. Now we have a labor surplus, because even though our population growth has been fairly slow since the middle of the century, the growth of labor-eliminating mechanical devices and processes has been quite rapid, even exponential. Therefore to volunteer for this kind of total donation is considered a deed of the highest social utility, removing as it does a healthy young body from the overcrowded labor force and at the same time providing some elder statesman with the assurance that the supply of vital organs will not unduly diminish. Of course you have to be crazy to volunteer, but there's never been any shortage of lunatics in our society.

If you're not drafted by the age of twenty-one, through some lucky fluke, you're safe. And a few of us do slip through the net, I'm told. So far there are more of us in the total draft pool than there are patients in need of transplants. But the ratios are changing rapidly. The draft legislation is still relatively new. Before long they'll have drained the pool of eligible draftees, and then what? Birth rates nowadays are low; the supply of potential draftees is finite. But death rates are even lower; the demand for organs is essentially infinite. I can give you only one of my kidneys, if I am to survive; but you, as you live on and on, may require more than one kidney transplant. Some recipients may need five or six sets of kidneys or lungs before they finally get beyond the hope of repair at age one-seventy or so. As those who've given organs come to requisition organs later on in life, the pressure on the under-twenty-one group will get even greater. Those in need of transplants will come to outnumber those who can donate organs, and everybody in the pool will get clipped. And then? Well, they could lower the draft age to seventeen or sixteen or even fourteen. But even that's only a short-term solution. Sooner or later, there won't be enough spare organs to go around.

Will I stay? Will I flee? Will I go to court? Time's running out. My call is sure to come up in another few weeks. I feel a tickling sensation in my back, now and then, as though somebody's quietly sawing at my kidneys.

Cannibalism. At Chou-kou-tien, Dragon Bone Hill, 25 miles southwest of Peking, paleontologists excavating a cave early in the twentieth century discovered the fossil skulls of Peking Man, *Pithacanthropus pekinensis*. The skulls had been broken away at the base, which led Franz Weidenreich, the director of the Dragon Bone Hill digs, to speculate that Peking Man was a cannibal who had killed his own kind, extracted the brains of his victims through openings in the base of their skulls, cooked and feasted on the cerebral meat—there were hearths and fragments of charcoal at the site—and left the skulls behind in the cave as trophies. To eat your enemy's flesh: to absorb his skills, his strengths, his knowledge, his achievements, his virtues. It took mankind five hundred thousand years to struggle upward from cannibalism. But we never lost the old craving, did we? There's still easy comfort to gain by devouring those who are younger, stronger, more agile than you. We've improved the techniques, is all. And so now they eat us raw, the old ones, they gobble us up, organ by throbbing organ. Is that really an improvement? At least Peking Man cooked his meat.

Our brave new society, where all share equally in the triumphs of medicine, and the deserving senior citizens need not feel that their merits and prestige will be rewarded only by a cold grave—we sing its praises all the time. How pleased everyone is about the organ draft: except, of course, a few disgruntled draftees.

The ticklish question of priorities. Who gets the stockpiled organs? They have an elaborate system by which hierarchies are defined. Supposedly a big computer drew it up, thus ensuring absolute godlike impartiality. You earn salvation through good works: accomplishments in career and benevolence in daily life win you points that nudge you up the ladder until you reach one of the high-priority classifications, 4-G or better. No doubt the classification system is impartial and is administered justly. But is it rational? Whose needs does it serve? In 1943, during World War II, there was a shortage of the newly discovered drug penicillin among the American military forces in North Africa. Two groups of soldiers were most in need of its benefits: those who were suffering from infected battle wounds and those who had contracted venereal disease. A junior medical officer, working from self-evident moral principles, ruled that the wounded heroes were more deserving of treatment than the self-indulgent syphilitics. He was overruled by the medical officer in charge, who observed that the VD cases could be restored to active duty more quickly, if treated; besides, if they remained untreated they served as vectors of further infection. Therefore, he gave them the penicillin and left the wounded groaning on their beds of pain. The logic of the battlefield, incontrovertible, unassailable.

The great chain of life. Little creatures in the plankton are eaten by larger ones, and the greater plankton falls prey to little fishes, and little fishes to bigger fishes, and so on up to the tuna and the dolphin and the shark. I eat the flesh of the tuna and I thrive and flourish and grow fat, and store up energy in my vital organs. And am eaten in turn by the shriveled wizened seniors. All life is linked. I see my destiny.

In the early days rejection of the transplanted organ was the big problem. Such a waste! The body failed to distinguish between a beneficial though alien organ and an intrusive, hostile microorganism. The mechanism known as the immune response was mobilized to drive out the invader. At the point of invasion enzymes came into play, a brush-fire war designed to rip down and dissolve the foreign substances. White corpuscles poured in via the circulatory system, vigilant phagocytes on the march. Through the lymphatic network came antibodies, high-powered protein missiles. Before any technology of organ grafts could be developed, methods had to be devised to suppress the immune response. Drugs, radiation treatment, metabolic shock—one way and another, the organ-rejection problem was long ago conquered. I can't conquer my draft-rejection problem. Aged and rapacious legislators, I reject you and your legislation.

My call notice came today. They'll need one of my kidneys. The usual request. "You're lucky," somebody said at lunchtime. "They might have wanted a lung."

Kate and I walk into the green glistening hills and stand among the blossoming oleanders and corianders and frangipani and whatever. How good it is to be alive, to breathe this fragrance, to show our bodies to the bright sun! Her skin is tawny and glowing. Her beauty makes me weep. She will not be spared. None of us will be spared. I go first, then she, or is it she ahead of me? Where will they make the incision? Here, on her smooth rounded back? Here, on the flat taut belly? I can see the high priest standing over the altar. At the first blaze of dawn his shadow falls across her. The obsidian knife that is clutched in his upraised hand has a terrible fiery sparkle. The choir offers up a discordant hymn to the god of blood. The knife descends.

My last chance to escape across the border. I've been up all night, weighing the options. There's no hope of appeal. Running away leaves a bad taste in my mouth. Father, friends, even Kate, all say stay, stay, stay, face the music. The hour of decision. Do I really have a choice? I have no choice. When the time comes, I'll surrender peacefully.

I report to Transplant House for conscriptive donative surgery in three hours.

"After all," he said coolly, "what's a kidney?" I'll still have another one, you know. And if that one malfunctions, I can always get a replacement. I'll have Preferred Recipient status, 6-A, for what that's worth. But I won't settle for my automatic 6-A. I know what's going to happen to the priority system; I'd better protect myself. I'll go into politics. I'll climb. I'll attain upward mobility out of enlightened self-interest, right? Right. I'll become so important that society will owe me a thousand transplants. And one of these years I'll get that kidney back. Three or four kidneys, fifty kidneys, as many as I need. A heart or two. A few lungs. A pancreas, a spleen, a liver. They won't be able to refuse me anything. I'll show them. I'll show them. I'll out-senior the seniors. There's your Bodily Sanctity activist for you, eh? I suppose I'll have to resign from the League. Good-bye, idealism. Good-bye, moral superiority. Good-bye, kidney. Good-bye, good-bye, good-bye.

It's done. I've paid my debt to society. I've given up unto the powers that be my humble pound of flesh. When I leave the hospital in a couple of days, I'll carry a card testifying to my new 6-A status.

Top priority for the rest of my life.

Why, I might live for a thousand years.

Neutral Planet

From the fore viewing bay of the Terran starship *Peccable,* the twin planets Fasolt and Fafnir had become visible—uninhabited Fasolt a violet ball the size of a quarter-credit piece dead ahead, and Fafnir, home of the gnorphs, a bright-red dot far to the right, beyond the mighty curve of the big ship's out-sweeping wing.

The nameless, tiny blue sun about which both worlds orbited rode high above them, at a sharp 36° off the ecliptic. And, majestic in its vastness, great Antares served as a huge bright-red backdrop for the entire scene.

"Fasolt dead ahead," came the word from Navigation. "Prepare for decelerating orbit."

The eighteen men who comprised the Terran mission to the gnorphs of Fafnir moved rapidly and smoothly toward their landing stations. This was a functioning team; they had a big job, and they were ready for it.

In Control Cabin, Shipmaster Deev Harskin was strapping himself into the acceleration cradle when the voice of Observer First Rank Snollgren broke in.

"Chief? Snollgren. Read me?"

"Go ahead, boy. What's up?"

"That Rigellian ship—the one we saw yesterday? I just found it again. Ten light-seconds off starboard, and credits to crawfish it's orbiting in on Fasolt!"

Harskin gripped the side of the cradle anxiously. "You sure it's not Fafnir they're heading for? How's your depth-perception out there?"

"A-one. That boat's going the same place we are, Chief!"

Sighing, Harskin said, "It could have been worse, I guess." He snapped on the all-ship communicator and said, "Gentlemen, our job has been complicated somewhat. Observer Snollgren reports a Rigellian ship orbiting in on Fasolt, and it looks likely they have the same idea we have. Well, this'll be a test of our mettle. We'll have a chance to snatch Fafnir right out from under their alleged noses!"

A voice said, "Why not blast the Rigellians first? They're our enemies, aren't they?"

Harskin recognized the voice as belonging to Leefman —a first-rate linguist, rather innocent of the niceties of interstellar protocol. No reply from Harskin was needed. The hoarse voice of Military Attaché Ramos broke in.

"This is a neutral system, Leefman. Rigellian-Terran hostilities are suspended pending contact with the gnorphs. Someday you'll understand that war has its code too."

Alone in Control Cabin, Shipmaster Harskin smiled. It was a good crew; a little overspecialized, perhaps, but more than adequate for the purpose. Having Rigellians on hand would be just so much additional challenge. Shipmaster Harskin enjoyed challenges.

Beneath him, the engines of the *Peccable* throbbed magnificently. He was proud of his ship, proud of his crew. The *Peccable* swept into the deadly atmosphere of Fasolt, swung downward in big looping spirals, and headed for land.

Not too far behind came the Rigellians. Harskin leaned back and let the crash of deceleration eddy up over him, and waited.

Fasolt was mostly rock, except for the hydrogen-fluoride oceans and the hydrogenous air. It was not an appealing planet.

The space-suited men of the *Peccable* were quick to debouch and extrude their dome. Atmosphere issued into it. "A little home away from home," Harskin remarked.

Biochemist Carver squinted balefully at the choppy hydrofluoric-acid sea. "Nice world. Good thing these goldfish bowls aren't made out of glass, yes? And better caution your men about using the dome airlock. A little of our oxygen gets out into that atmosphere and we'll have the loveliest rainstorm you ever want to see—with us a thousand feet up, looking down."

Harskin nodded. "It's not a pleasant place at all. But it's not a pleasant war we're fighting."

He glanced up at the murky sky. Fafnir was full, a broad red globe barely a million miles away. And, completing the group, there was the faint blue sun about which both worlds revolved, the entire system forming a neat Trojan equilateral with vast Antares.

Snollgren appeared. The keen-eyed Observer had been in the ship, and apparently had made it from the *Peccable* to the endomed temporary camp on a dead run, no little feat in Fasolt's 1.5 g field.

"Well?" Harskin asked.

The Observer opened his faceplate and sucked in some of the dome's high-oxygen atmosphere. "The Rigellians," he gasped. "They've landed. I saw them in orbit."

"Where?"

"I'd estimate five hundred miles westward. They're definitely on this continent."

Harskin glanced at the chronometer set in the wrist of Snollgren's space suit. "We'll give them an hour to set up their camp. Then we'll contact them and find out what goes."

The Rigellian captain's name was Fourteen Deathless. He spoke Galactic with a sharp, crisp accent that Harskin attributed to his ursine ancestry.

"Coincidence we're both here at the same time, eh, Shipmaster Harskin? Strange are the ways of the Guiding Forces."

"They certainly are," Harskin said. He stared at the hand-mike, wishing it were a screen so he could see the sly, smug expression on the Rigellian's furry face. Obviously, someone had intercepted Harskin's allegedly secret orders and studied them carefully before forwarding them to their recipient.

Coincidences didn't happen in interstellar war. The Rigellians were here because they knew the Earthmen were.

"We have arrived at a knotty problem in ethics," remarked Captain Fourteen Deathless. "Both of us are here for the same purpose, that of negotiating trading rights with the gnorphs. Now—ah—which of us is to make the first attempt to deal with these people?"

"Obviously," said Harskin, "the ship which landed on Fasolt first has prior claim."

"This is suitable," said the Rigellian.

"We'll leave at once, then. Since the *Peccable* landed at least half an hour before your ship, we have clear priority."

"Interesting," Captain Fourteen Deathless said. "But just how do you compute you arrived before we did? By our instruments we were down long before you."

Harskin started to sputter, then checked himself. "Impossible!"

"Oh? Cite your landing time, please, with reference to Galactic Absolute."

"We put down at . . ." Harskin paused. "No. Suppose *you* tell *me* what time *you* landed, and then I'll give you our figures."

"That's hardly fair," said the Rigellian. "How do we know you won't alter your figures once we've given ours?"

"And how do *we* know, on the other hand . . . ?"

"It won't work," said the alien. "Neither of us will allow the other priority."

Shrugging, Harskin saw the truth of that. Regardless of the fact that the *Peccable* actually *had* landed first, the Rigellians would never admit it. It was a problem in simple relativity; without an external observer to supply impartial data, it was Fourteen Deathless' word against Harskin's. It was impossible to prove to the Rigellian that he was lying—and therefore, he wasn't lying!

"All right," Harskin said wearily. "Call it a stalemate. Suppose we *both* go to Fafnir now, and have them choose between us."

There was silence at the other end for a while. Then the Rigellian said, "This is acceptable. The rights of the neutral parties must be respected, of course."

"Of course. Until this system is settled, we're *all* neutrals, remember?"

"Naturally," said the Rigellian.

It was not, thought Harskin, a totally satisfactory arrangement. Still, it could hardly be helped.

By the very strict rules with which the Terran-Rigellian "war" was being fought, a system was considered neutral until a majority of its intelligently inhabited worlds had declared a preference for one power or the other.

In the Antares system, a majority vote would have to be a unanimous one. Of the eleven highly variegated

worlds that circled the giant red star, only Fafnir bore
life. The gnorphs were an intelligent race of biped hu-
manoids—the classic shape of intelligent life. The Terrans were simianoid; the Rigellians, ursinoid. But the
gnorphs owed their appearance neither to apes nor
bears; they were reptilians, erect and tailless. Fafnir was
not hospitable to mammalian life.

Harskin stared broodingly out the viewing bay as the
blood-red seas of Fafnir grew larger. The Rigellian ship
could not be seen, but he knew it was on its way. He
made a mental note to inform Terran Intelligence that
the secrecy of the high command's secret orders was
open to some question.

It was a strange war—a war fought with documents
rather than energy cannons. The shooting stage of the
war between the galaxy's two leading races had long
since ended in sheer futility; the development of the
Martineau Negascreen, which happily drank up every
megawatt of a bombardment and fired it back at
triple intensity, had quickly put an end to active hostility.

Now, the war was carried on at a subtler level—the
economic one. Rigal and Terra strove to outdo each other
in extracting exclusive trading rights from systems, hoping to choke each other's lifelines. The universe was infinite, or close enough to infinite to keep both systems
busy for quite a few millennia to come.

Harskin shrugged. Terran scouts had visited Fafnir
and had reported little anxiety on the part of the gnorphs
to take part in the Galactic stream of things. Presumably,
Rigel IV had not yet visited the world; it was simpler to
pirate the Terran scout reports.

Well, this would really be a test.

"Preparing to land, sir," said Navigator Dominic. "Any
instructions?"

"Yes," Harskin said. "Bring us down where it's dry."

The landing was a good one, on the centermost of the island group that made up Fafnir's main land mass. Harskin and his twelve men—he had left five behind in the dome on Fasolt to hedge his bet—left the ship.

It would not be necessary to erect a dome here; Fafnir's air was breathable, more or less. It was 11 per cent oxygen, 86 per cent nitrogen, and a whopping 3 per cent of inerts, but a decent filter system easily strained the excess nitro and argon out and pumped in oxygen.

Wearing breathing-masks and converters, the thirteen Terrans advanced inland. At their backs was the ocean, red and glimmering in Antares' light.

"Here come the Rigellians," Observer Snollgren cried.

"As usual, they're hanging back and waiting to see what we do." Harskin frowned. "This time, we won't wait for them. Let's take advantage of our head start."

The gnorph village was five miles inland, but the party had not gone more than two miles when they were greeted by a group of aliens.

There were about a hundred of them, advancing in a wedge-shaped phalanx. They were moving slowly, without any overt belligerent ideas, but Harskin felt uneasy. A hundred aroused savages could make quick work of thirteen Terrans armed with handguns.

He glanced at Mawley, Contact Technician First Class. "Go ahead. Get up there and tell 'em we're friends."

Mawley was a tall redhead with knobby cheekbones and, at the moment, an expression of grave self-concern. He nodded, checked his lingual converter to make sure it was operating, and stepped forward, one hand upraised.

"Greetings," he said loudly. "We come in peace."

The gnorphs spread out into a loose formation and stared stolidly ahead. Harskin, waiting tensely for Mawley to achieve his rapport with the aliens, peered curiously at them.

They were short—five-six or so—and correspondingly broad-beamed. Their chocolate-brown skin was glossy and scaled; it hung loosely, in corrugated folds. Thick antennae twined upward from either side of their bald heads, and equally thick fleshy processes dangled comblike from their jaws. As for their eyes, Harskin was unable to see them; they were hidden in deep shadow, set back two inches in their skull and protected by projecting, brooding rims of bone that circled completely around each eye.

Three of the gnorphs stepped out of the ranks, and the middle alien stepped forward, flanked slightly to the rear by his companions. He spoke in a harsh, guttural voice.

The converter rendered it as "What do you want here?"

Mawley was prepared for the question. "Friendship. Peace. Mutual happiness of our worlds."

"Where are you from?"

Mawley gestured to the sky. "Far away, beyond the sky. Beyond the stars. Much distance."

The gnorph looked skeptical. "How many days' sailing from here?"

"Many days. Many, *many* days."

"Then why come to us?"

"To establish friendship," said Mawley. "To build a bond between your world and ours."

At that, the alien did an abrupt about-face and conferred with his two companions. Harskin kept an eye on the spears twitching in the alien hands.

The conference seemed to be prolonging itself indefinitely. Mawley glanced back at Harskin as if to ask what he should do next, but the Shipmaster merely smiled in approval and encouragement.

Finally the aliens broke up their huddle and the lead man turned back to the Terrans. "We think you should leave us," he grunted. "Go. At once."

There was nothing in Mawley's instructions to cover this. The Contact Technician opened and closed his mouth a few times without speaking. Gravely, the aliens turned and marched away, leaving the Terrans alone.

First Contact had been achieved.

"This has to be done in a very careful way," Harskin said. "Any news from the Rigellians?"

"They're situated about eight miles from here," Snollgren said.

"Hmm. That means they're as far from the village as we are." Harskin put his hands to his head. "The gnorphs are certainly not leaping all over the place to sign a treaty with us, that's for sure. We'll have to handle them gently or we may make them angry enough to sign up with the Rigellians."

"I doubt that," offered Sociologist Yang. "They probably won't be any more anxious to deal with the Rigellians than they are with us. They're neutrals, and they want to stay that way."

Harskin leaned back. "This is a problem we haven't hit before. None of the worlds in either sphere of influence ever had any isolationist ideas. What do we do? Just pull up and leave?"

The blue sun was setting. Antares still hovered on the horizon, a shapeless blob of pale red eating up half the sky. "We'll have to send a man to spy on the Rigellians. Archer, you're elected."

The man in question rose. "Yes, sir."

"Keep an eye on them, watch their dealings with the gnorphs, and above all don't let the Rigellians see you." Another idea occurred to the Shipmaster. "Lloyd?"

"Yes, sir?"

"In all probability the Rigellians have slapped a spy on *us*. You're our counterespionage man, effective now. Scout around and see if you can turn up their spy."

Archer and Lloyd departed. Harskin turned to the Sociologist. "Yang, there has to be some way of pushing these gnorphs to one side or the other."

"Agreed. I'll have to see more of the pattern, though, before I can help you."

Harskin nodded. "We'll make contact with the gnorphs again after Archer returns with word of what the Rigellians are up to. We'll profit by their mistakes."

Antares had set as far as it was going to set, which was about three quarters of the way below the horizon, and the blue sun was spiraling its way into the heavens again, when the quiet air of Fafnir was split by an earth-shaking explosion.

The men of the *Peccable* were awake in an instant— those eight who had been sleeping, at any rate. A two-man skeleton team had been guarding the ship. Harskin had been meditating in Control Cabin, and Archer and Lloyd had not yet returned from their scouting missions.

Almost simultaneously with the explosion came the clangor of the alarm bell at the main airlock, signifying someone wanted in. A moment later, Observer First Class Snollgren was on the wire, excitedly jabbering something incoherent.

Harskin switched on the all-ship communicator and yelled, "*Stop! Whoa! Halt!*"

There was silence. He said, "Clyde, see what's going on at the airlock. Snollgren, slow down and tell me what you just saw."

"It was the Rigellian ship, sir!" the Observer said. "It just left. That was the noise we heard."

"You sure of that?"

"Double positive. It took off in one hell of a hurry and I caught it on a tangent bound out of here."

"Okay. Clyde, what's at the airlock?"

"It's Lloyd, sir. He's back, and he's got a Rigellian prisoner with him."

"Prisoner? What the—all right, have them both come up here."

Radioman Klaristenfeld was next on the line. He said, "Sir, report coming in from the base on Fasolt. They confirm blast-off of a ship from Fafnir. They thought it might be us."

"Tell the idiots it isn't," Harskin snapped. "And tell them to watch out for the Rigellian ship. It's probably on its way back to Fasolt."

The door-annunciator chimed. Harskin pressed *admit* and Lloyd entered, preceded at blaster-point by a very angry-looking Rigellian.

"Where'd you find him?" Harskin asked.

"Mousing around near the ship," said Lloyd. The thin spaceman was pale and tense-looking. "I was patrolling the area as you suggested when I heard the explosion. I looked up and saw the Rigellian ship up overhead and heading outward. And then this guy came crashing out of the underbrush and started cursing a blue streak in Rigellian. He didn't even see me until I had the blaster pointing in his face."

Harskin glanced at the Rigellian. "What's your name and rank, Rigellian?"

"Three Ninety-Seven Indomitable," the alien said. He was a formidably burly seven-footer, covered with stiff, coarse black hair and wearing a light-yellow leather harness. His eyes glinted coldly. He looked angry. "Espionage man first order," he said.

"That explains what you were doing near our ship, then, Three Ninety-Seven Indomitable," Harskin said. "What can you tell me about this quick blast-off?"

"Not a thing. The first I knew of it was when it happened. They marooned me! They left me here!" The alien slipped from Galactic into a Rigellian tongue and growled what must have been some highly picturesque profanity.

"They just *left* you?" Harskin repeated in amazement. "Something must have made them decide to clear out of here in an awful hurry, then." He turned to Lloyd. "Convey the prisoner to the brig and see that he's put there to stay. Then pick two men and start combing the countryside for Archer. I want to know what made the Rigellians get out of here so fast they didn't have time to pick up their own spy."

As it developed, very little countryside combing was necessary to locate Archer. Harskin's spy returned to the *Peccable* about three quarters of an hour later, extremely winded after his long cross-country trot.

It took him five minutes to calm down enough to deliver his report.

"I tracked the Rigellians back to their ship," he said. "They were all gathered around it, and I waited in the underbrush. After a while they proceeded to the gnorph village, and I followed them."

"Any attempt at counterespionage?" Harskin asked.

"Yes, sir." Archer grinned uncomfortably. "I killed him."

Harskin nodded. "Go on."

"They reached the village. I stayed about thirty yards behind them and switched on my converter so I could hear what they were saying."

"Bad, but unavoidable," Harskin said. "They might have had a man at the ship tracing the energy flow. I guess they didn't, though. What happened in the village?"

"They introduced themselves, and gave the usual line —the same thing we said, about peace and friendship and stuff. Then they started handing out gifts. Captain Fourteen Deathless said this was to cement Rigel's friendship with Fafnir—only he didn't call it Fafnir, naturally.

"They handed mirrors all around, and little forcewave generators, and all sorts of trinkets and gadgets. The gnorphs took each one and stacked it in a heap off to one side. The Rigellians kept handing out more and more, and the stack kept growing. Then, finally, Fourteen Deathless said he felt the gifts had been sufficient. He started to explain the nature of the treaty. And one of the gnorphs stepped out and pointed to the stack of gifts. 'Are you quite finished delivering things?' he asked, in a very stuffy tone. The Rigellian looked flustered and said more gifts would be forthcoming after the treaty was signed. And that blew the roof off."

"How do you mean?"

"It happened so fast I'm not sure. But suddenly all the gnorphs started waving their spears and looking menacing, and then someone threw a spear at a Rigellian. That started it. The Rigellians had some handguns with them, but they were so close they hardly had a chance to use them. It was a real massacre. About half the Rigellians escaped, including Captain Deathless. I hid in the underbrush till it was all over. Then I came back here."

Harskin looked at Sociologist Yang. "Well? What do you make of it?"

"Obviously a greedy sort of culture," the Sociologist remarked. "The Rigellians made the mistake of being too stingy. I suggest we wait till morning and go to that village ourselves, and shoot the works. With the Rigellians gone we've got a clear field, and if we're liberal enough the planet will be ours."

"Don't be too sure of that," Harskin said broodingly. "That Rigellian was no bigger a fool than I am. When we go to that village, we'll go well armed."

The gnorph village was a cluster of thatched huts set in a wide semicircle over some extremely marshy swampland. Both Antares and the blue companion were in the sky when the Earthmen arrived; Fasolt was making its daily occultation of the giant sun.

Harskin had taken six of his men with him: Yang, Leefman, Archer, Mawley, Ramos, and Carver. Six more remained at the ship, seeing to it that the *Peccable* was primed for a quick getaway, if necessary.

The gifts of the Rigellians lay in a scattered heap in the center of the village, smashed and battered. Nearby lay half a dozen mutilated Rigellian bodies. Harskin shuddered despite himself; these gnorphs were cold-blooded in more than the literal biological sense!

A group of them filtered out of their huts and confronted the approaching Earthmen. In the mingled blue-and-red light of the two suns—one huge and dim, the other small and dim—the blank, scaly faces looked strange and menacing, the bone-hooded eye sockets cold and ugly.

"What do you want here, strangers?"

"We have come to thank you," Mawley said, "for killing our enemies, the fur-men." He had been instructed to stress the distinction between the group of Rigellians and the Earthmen. "The fur-men were here last night, bearing niggling gifts. They are our enemies. We of Earth offer you peace and goodwill."

The gnorphs stared squarely at the tense little party

of Earthmen. Each of the seven Terrans carried a powerful blaster set for wide-beam stunning, highly efficient if not particularly deadly as a close-range weapon. In the event of a battle, the Earthmen would at least be ready.

"What is it you want here?" the gnorph leader asked with thinly concealed impatience.

"We wish to sign a treaty between your world and ours," said Mawley. "A bond of eternal friendship, of loyalty and fellowship between worlds."

Somewhere in the distance an unseen beast emitted a rumbling reptilian honk—quite spoiling the effect, Harskin thought.

"Friendship? Fellowship?" the gnorph repeated, indicating by a quivering shake of his wattles that these were difficult concepts for him to grasp.

"Yes," said Mawley. "And as signs of our friendship we bring you gifts—not piddling trinkets such as our enemies foisted on you last night, but gifts of incomparable richness, gifts which will be just part of the bounty to fall upon you if you will sign with us."

At a signal from Harskin, they began unloading the gifts they had brought with them: miniaturized cameras, game-detectors, dozens of other treasures calculated to impress the gnorphs.

And then it began.

Harskin had been on the lookout for the explosion ever since they had arrived, and when he saw the spears beginning to bristle in the gnorph ranks, he yanked his blaster out and fired.

The stunning beam swept the front rank of gnorphs; they fell. The others growled menacingly and advanced.

The seven Earthmen jammed together in a unit and fired constantly; gnorphs lay unconscious all over, and still more came pouring from the huts. The Terrans started to run. Spears sailed past their heads.

It was a long, grim retreat to the ship.

They were still a quarter of a million miles from Fasolt when Radioman Klaristenfeld reported that Captain Fourteen Deathless of the Rigellian ship was calling.

"We see you have left also," the Rigellian said when Harskin took the phone. "You were evidently as unsuccessful as we."

"Not quite," Harskin said. "At least we got out of there without any casualties. I counted six dead Rigellians outside that village—plus the man you left behind to watch over us. He's in our brig."

"Ah. I had wondered what became of him. Well, Harskin, do we declare Fafnir a neutral planet and leave it at that? It's a rather unsatisfactory finish to our little encounter."

"Agreed. But what can we do? We dumped nearly fifty thousand credits' worth of trinkets when we escaped."

"You Terrans are lavish," the Rigellian observed. "Our goods were worth but half that."

"That's the way it goes," Harskin said. "Well, best wishes, Fourteen Deathless."

"One moment! Is the decision a dual withdrawal?"

"I'm not so sure," Harskin said, and broke the contact.

When they reached Fasolt and rejoined the men in the dome, Harskin ordered a general meeting. He had an idea.

"The aliens," he said, "offered the gnorphs twenty-five thousand credits of goods, and were repulsed angrily. We offered twice as much—and, if Archer's account of the Rigellian incident was accurate, we were repulsed about twice as fast. Yang, does that suggest anything to you?"

The little Sociologist wrinkled his head. "The pattern still is not clear," he said.

"I didn't think so." Harskin knotted his fingers in concentration. "Let me put it this way: the degree of insult the gnorphs felt was in direct variance with the degree of wealth offered. That sound plausible?"

Yang nodded.

"Tell me: what happens when an isolated, biologically glum race is visited by warm-blooded aliens from the skies? Suppose those warm-blooded aliens want a treaty of friendship—and offer to *pay* for it? How will the natives react, Yang?"

"I see. They'll get highly insulted. We're treating them in a cavalier fashion."

"More than that. We're obliging them to us. We're *purchasing* that treaty with our gifts. But obviously gifts are worth more than a treaty of friendship, so they feel they'll still owe us something if they accept. They don't want to owe us anything. So they chase us away.

"Now," continued Harskin, "if we reverse the situation —if we make ourselves beholden to them, and *beg* for the signing of the treaty instead of trying to *buy* a treaty —why, that gives them a chance to seem lordly." He turned to Ramos, the Military Attaché. "Ramos, do you think a solar system is worth a spaceship?"

"Eh?"

"I mean, if it becomes necessary to sacrifice our ship in order to win the Antares system, will that be a strategically sound move?"

"I imagine so," Ramos said cautiously.

Harskin flicked a bead of sweat from his forehead. "Very well, then. Mawley, you and I and Navigator Dominic are going to take the *Peccable* on her final cruise. Klaristenfeld, I want you to get a subradio sending set inside my space suit, and make damned sure you don't put it where it'll bother me. Snollgren, you monitor the area and keep me posted on what the Rigellians are doing, if anything."

He pointed to the Navigator. "Come up to Control Cabin, Dominic. We're going to work out the most precise orbit you'll ever need to compute."

Antares was sinking in the sky and the blue sun was in partial eclipse. Suddenly, the *Peccable* flashed across the sky of Fafnir, trailing smoke at both jets, roaring like a wounded giant as it circled in wildly for its crash landing.

The three men aboard were huddled in their acceleration cradles, groaning in pain as the increasing grav buffeted and bruised them. Below, Fafnir sprang up to meet the ship.

Harskin was bathed in his own sweat. So many things could go wrong. . . .

They might have computed one tenth-place decimal awry—and would land square in the heart of the swampland.

The stabilizer jets might be consumed by the blaze they had set too soon, and the impact of their landing would kill them.

The airlock might refuse to open.

The gnorphs might fail to act as expected. . . .

It was, he thought, an insane venture.

The ship throbbed suddenly as the stabilizer jets went into action. The *Peccable* froze for a fraction of a second, then began to glide.

It struck the blood-red ocean nose first. Furiously, Harskin climbed from his cradle and into his space suit. *Now, if we only figured the buoyancy factor right . . .*

Two space-suited figures waited for him at the airlock. He grinned at them, threw open the hatch, and stepped into the outer chamber. The door opened; a wall of water rushed at him. He squirted out of the sinking ship and popped to the surface like a cork. A moment later he saw Mawley and Dominic come bobbing above the water nearby.

He turned. All that was visible of the *Peccable* was the rear jet assembly and the tips of the once-proud wings. An oily slick was starting to cover the bright-red water. The ship was sinking rapidly as water poured into the lock.

"Look over there!" Mawley exclaimed.

Harskin looked. Something that looked like a small island with a neck was approaching him: a monstrous turtle-like thing with a thick, saurian neck and a crested unintelligent head, from which dangled seven or eight fleshy barbels.

And riding in a sort of howdah erected on the broad carapace were three gnorphs, peering curiously at the three space-suited men bobbing in the water.

The rescue party was on time.

"Help!" cried Harskin. "Rescue us! Oh, I beg of you, rescue us, and we'll be eternally obliged to you! Rescue us!"

He hoped the converter was translating the words with a suitable inflection of piteous despair.

DOUBLEPLUS PRIORITY 03–16–2952 ABS XPF32
EXP FORCE ANTARES SYSTEM TO HIGH COMMAND TERRA:
BE ADVISED ANTARES SYSTEM IN TERRAN FOLD. RIGEL-LIANS ON HAND HAVE VALIDATED OUR TREATY WITH IN-HABITANTS OF FAFNIR ANTARES' ONE WORLD. ALL IS WELL AND NO CASUALTIES EXCEPT SHIP PECCABLE ACCIDEN-TALLY DESTROYED. FIFTEEN MEMBERS OF CREW LIVING IN DOME ON COMPANION WORLD FASOLT, THREE OF US LIV-ING ON FAFNIR. PLEASE SEND PICKUP SHIP DOUBLE FAST AS WE ARE CURRENTLY IN MENIAL SERVITUDE.
ALL THE BEST, LOVE AND KISSES, ETC.

HARSKIN

The Pain Peddlers

Pain Is Gain
—Greek Proverb

The phone bleeped. Northrop nudged the cut-in switch and heard Maurillo say, "We got a gangrene, Chief. They're amputating tonight."

Northrop's pulse quickened at the thought of action. "What's the tab?" he asked.

"Five thousand, all rights."

"Anesthetic?"

"Natch," Maurillo said. "I tried it the other way."

"What did you offer?"

"Ten. It was no go."

Northrop sighed. "I'll have to handle it myself, I guess. Where's the patient?"

"Clinton General. In the wards."

Northrop raised a heavy eyebrow and glowered into the screen. "In the *wards*?" he bellowed. "And you couldn't get them to agree?"

Maurillo seemed to shrink. "It was the relatives, Chief. They were stubborn. The old man, he didn't seem to give a damn, but the relatives—"

"Okay. You stay there. I'm coming over to close the deal," Northrop snapped. He cut the phone out and pulled a couple of blank waiver forms out of his desk, just in case the relatives backed down. Gangrene was gangrene, but ten grand was ten grand. And business was business. The networks were yelling. He had to supply the goods or get out.

95

He thumbed the autosecretary. "I want my car ready in thirty seconds. South Street exit."

"Yes, Mr. Northrop."

"If anyone calls for me in the next half hour, record it. I'm going to Clinton General Hospital, but I don't want to be called there."

"Yes, Mr. Northrop."

"If Rayfield calls from the network office, tell him I'm getting him a dandy. Tell him—oh, hell, tell him I'll call him back in an hour. That's all."

"Yes, Mr. Northrop."

Northrop scowled at the machine and left his office. The gravshaft took him down forty stories in almost literally no time flat. His car was waiting, as ordered, a long, sleek '08 Frontenac with bubble top. Bullet-proof, of course. Network producers were vulnerable to crackpot attacks.

He sat back, nestling into the plush upholstery. The car asked him where he was going, and he answered.

"Let's have a pep pill," he said.

A pill rolled out of the dispenser in front of him. He gulped it down. *Maurillo, you make me sick,* he thought. *Why can't you close a deal without me? Just once?*

He made a mental note. Maurillo had to go. The organization couldn't tolerate inefficiency.

The hospital was an old one. It was housed in one of the vulgar green-glass architectural monstrosities so popular sixty years before, a tasteless slab-sided thing without character or grace. The main door irised and Northrop stepped through, and the familiar hospital smell hit his nostrils. Most people found it unpleasant, but not Northrop. It was the smell of dollars, for him.

The hospital was so old that it still had nurses and

orderlies. Oh, plenty of mechanicals skittered up and down the corridors, but here and there a middle-aged nurse, smugly clinging to her tenure, pushed a tray of mush along, or a doddering orderly propelled a broom. In his early days on video, Northrop had done a documentary on these people, these living fossils in the hospital corridors. He had won an award for the film, with its crosscuts from baggy-faced nurses to gleaming mechanicals, its vivid presentation of the inhumanity of the new hospitals. It was a long time since Northrop had done a documentary of that sort. A different kind of show was the order of the day now, ever since the intensifiers had come in.

A mechanical took him to Ward Seven. Maurillo was waiting there, a short, bouncy little man who wasn't bouncing much now, because he knew he had fumbled. Maurillo grinned up at Northrop, a hollow grin, and said, "You sure made it fast, Chief!"

"How long would it take for the competition to cut in?" Northrop countered. "Where's the patient?"

"Down by the end. You see where the curtain is? I had the curtain put up. To get in good with the heirs. The relatives, I mean."

"Fill me in," Northrop said. "Who's in charge?"

"The oldest son. Harry. Watch out for him. Greedy."

"Who isn't?" Northrop sighed. They were at the curtain, now. Maurillo parted it. All through the long ward, patients were stirring. Potential subjects for taping, all of them, Northrop thought. The world was so full of different kinds of sickness—and one sickness fed on another.

He stepped through the curtain. There was a man in the bed, drawn and gaunt, his hollow face greenish, stubbly. A mechanical stood next to the bed, with an intravenous tube running across and under the covers. The patient looked at least ninety. Knocking off ten years for the effects of illness still made him pretty old, Northrop thought.

He confronted the relatives.

There were eight of them. Five women, ranging from middle age down to teens. Three men, the oldest about fifty, the other two in their forties. Sons and daughters and nieces and granddaughters, Northrop figured.

He said gravely, "I know what a terrible tragedy this must be for all of you. A man in the prime of his life— head of a happy family . . ." Northrop stared at the patient. "But I know he'll pull through. I can see the strength in him."

The oldest relative said, "I'm Harry Gardner. I'm his son. You're from the network?"

"I'm the producer," Northrop said. "I don't ordinarily come in person, but my assistant told me what a great human situation there was here, what a brave person your father is . . ."

The man in the bed slept on. He looked bad.

Harry Gardner said, "We made an arrangement. Five thousand bucks. We wouldn't do it, except for the hospital bills. They can really wreck you."

"I understand perfectly," Northrop said in his most unctuous tones. "That's why we're prepared to raise our offer. We're well aware of the disastrous effects of hospitalization on a small family, even today, in these times of protection. And so we can offer—"

"No! There's got to be anesthetic!" It was one of the daughters, a round, drab woman with colorless thin lips. "We ain't going to let you make him suffer!"

Northrop smiled. "It would only be a moment of pain for him. Believe me. We'd begin the anesthesia immediately after the amputation. Just let us capture that single instant of—"

"It ain't right! He's old, he's got to be given the best treatment! The pain could kill him!"

"On the contrary," Northrop said blandly. "Scientific research has shown that pain is often beneficial in amputation cases. It creates a nerve block, you see, that causes a kind of anesthesia of its own, without the harmful side effects of chemotherapy. And once the danger vectors are controlled, the normal anesthetic procedures can be invoked, and—" He took a deep breath, and went rolling glibly on to the crusher, "with the extra fee we'll provide, you can give your dear one the absolute finest in medical care. There'll be no reason to stint."

Wary glances were exchanged. Harry Gardner said, "How much are you offering?"

"May I see the leg?" Northrop countered.

The coverlet was peeled back. Northrop stared.

It was a nasty case. Northrop was no doctor, but he had been in this line of work for five years, and that was long enough to give him an amateur acquaintance with disease. He knew the old man was in bad shape. It looked as though there had been a severe burn, high up along the calf, which had probably been treated only with first aid. Then, in happy proletarian ignorance, the family had let the old man rot until he was gangrenous. Now the leg was blackened, glossy, and swollen from midcalf to the ends of the toes. Everything looked soft and decayed. Northrop had the feeling that he could reach out and break the puffy toes off, one at a time.

The patient wasn't going to survive. Amputation or not, he was probably rotten to the core by this time, and if the shock of amputation didn't do him in, general debilitation would. It was a good prospect for the show.

It was the kind of stomach-turning vicarious suffering that millions of viewers gobbled up avidly.

Northrop looked up and said, "Fifteen thousand if you'll allow a network-approved surgeon to amputate under our conditions. And we'll pay the surgeon's fee besides."

"Well . . ."

"And we'll also underwrite the entire cost of postoperative care for your father," Northrop added smoothly. "Even if he stays in the hospital for six months, we'll pay every nickel, over and above the telecast fee."

He had them. He could see the greed shining in their eyes. They were faced with bankruptcy, and he had come to rescue them, and did it matter all that much if the old man didn't have anesthetic when they sawed his leg off? He was hardly conscious even now. He wouldn't really feel a thing, not really.

Northrop produced the documents, the waivers, the contracts covering residuals and Latin-American reruns, the payment vouchers, all the paraphernalia. He sent Maurillo scuttling off for a secretary, and a few moments later a glistening mechanical was taking it all down.

"If you'll put your name here, Mr. Gardner . . ."

Northrop handed the pen to the eldest son. Signed, sealed, delivered.

"We'll operate tonight," Northrop said. "I'll send our surgeon over immediately. One of our best men. We'll give your father the care he deserves."

He pocketed the documents. It was done. Maybe it was barbaric to operate on an old man that way, Northrop thought, but he didn't bear the responsibility, after all. He was just giving the public what it wanted, and the public wanted spouting blood and tortured nerves. And what did it matter to the old man, really? Any experienced medic could tell you he was as good as dead. The operation wouldn't save him. Anesthesia wouldn't save him. If the gangrene didn't get him, postoperative shock would do him in. At worst, he would suffer only a few minutes under the knife, but at least his family would be free from the fear of financial ruin.

On the way out, Maurillo said, "Don't you think it's a little risky, Chief? Offering to pay the hospitalization expenses, I mean?"

"You've got to gamble a little sometimes to get what you want," Northrop said.

"Yeah, but that could run to fifty, sixty thousand! What'll that do to the budget?"

Northrop shrugged. "We'll survive. Which is more than the old man will. He can't make it through the night. We haven't risked a penny, Maurillo. Not a stinking cent."

Returning to the office, Northrup turned the papers on the Gardner amputation over to his assistants, set the wheels in motion for the show, and prepared to call it a day. There was only one bit of dirty work left to do. He had to fire Maurillo.

It wasn't called firing, of course. Maurillo had tenure, just like the hospital orderlies and everyone else below executive rank. It was more a demotion than anything else. Northrop had been increasingly dissatisfied with the little man's work for months, now, and today had been the clincher. Maurillo had no imagination. He didn't know how to close a deal. Why hadn't he thought of underwriting the hospitalization? *If I can't delegate responsibility to him,* Northrop told himself, *I can't use him at all.* There were plenty of other assistant producers in the outfit who'd be glad to step in.

Northrop spoke to a couple of them. He made his choice. A young fellow named Barton, who had been working on documentaries all year. Barton had done the plane-crash deal in London in the spring. He had a fine touch for the gruesome. He had been on hand at the World's Fair fire last year at Juneau. Yes, Barton was the man.

The next part was the sticky one. Northrop phoned Maurillo, even though Maurillo was only two rooms away —these things were never done in person—and said, "I've got some good news for you, Ted. We're shifting you to a new program."

"Shifting . . . ?"

"That's right. We had a talk in here this afternoon, and we decided you were being wasted on the blood and guts show. You need more scope for your talents. So we're moving you over to Kiddie Time. We think you'll really blossom there. You and Sam Kline and Ed Bragan ought to make a terrific team."

Northrop saw Maurillo's pudgy face crumble. The arithmetic was getting home; over here, Maurillo was Number Two, and on the new show, a much less important one, he'd be Number Three. It was a thumping boot downstairs, and Maurillo knew it.

The mores of the situation called for Maurillo to pretend he was receiving a rare honor. He didn't play the game. He squinted and said, "Just because I didn't sign up that old man's amputation?"

"What makes you think . . . ?"

"Three years I've been with you! Three years, and you kick me out just like that!"

"I told you, Ted, we thought this would be a big opportunity for you. It's a step up the ladder. It's—"

Maurillo's fleshy face puffed up with rage. "It's getting junked," he said bitterly. "Well, never mind, huh? It so happens I've got another offer. I'm quitting before you can can me. You can take your tenure and—"

Northrop blanked the screen.

The idiot, he thought. *The fat little idiot. Well, to hell with him!*

He cleared his desk, and cleared his mind of Ted Maurillo and his problems. Life was real, life was earnest. Maurillo just couldn't take the pace, that was all.

Northrop prepared to go home. It had been a long day.

At eight that evening came word that old Gardner was about to undergo the amputation. At ten, Northrop was phoned by the network's own head surgeon, Dr. Steele, with the news that the operation had failed.

"We lost him," Steele said in a flat, unconcerned voice. "We did our best, but he was a mess. Fibrillation set in, and his heart just ran away. Not a damned thing we could do."

"Did the leg come off?"

"Oh, sure. All this was *after* the operation."

"Did it get taped?"

"They're processing it now. I'm on my way out."

"Okay," Northrop said. "Thanks for calling."

"Sorry about the patient."

"Don't worry yourself," Northrop said. "It happens to the best of us."

The next morning, Northrop had a look at the rushes. The screening was in the Twenty-third Floor studio, and a select audience was on hand—Northrop, his new assistant producer Barton, a handful of network executives, a couple of men from the cutting room. Slick, bosomy girls handed out intensifier helmets—no mechanicals doing the work here!

Northrop slipped the helmet on over his head. He felt the familiar surge of excitement as the electrodes descended, as contact was made. He closed his eyes. There was a thrum of power somewhere in the room as the EEG-amplifier went into action. The screen brightened.

There was the old man. There was the gangrenous leg. There was Dr. Steele, crisp and rugged and dimple-chinned, the network's star surgeon, $250,000 a year's worth of talent. There was the scalpel, gleaming in Steele's hand.

Northrop began to sweat. The amplified brain waves were coming through the intensifier, and he felt the throbbing in the old man's leg, felt the dull haze of pain behind the old man's forehead, felt the weakness of being eighty years old and half dead.

Steele was checking out the electronic scalpel, now, while the nurses fussed around, preparing the man for the amputation. In the finished tape, there would be music, narration, all the trimmings, but now there was just a soundless series of images, and, of course, the tapped brainwaves of the sick man.

The leg was bare.

The scalpel descended.

Northrop winced as vicarious agony shot through him. He could feel the blazing pain, the brief searing hellishness as the scalpel slashed through diseased flesh and rotting bone. His whole body trembled, and he bit down hard on his lips and clenched his fists, and then it was over.

There was a cessation of pain. A catharsis. The leg no longer sent its pulsating messages to the weary brain. Now there was shock, the anesthesia of hyped-up pain, and with the shock came calmness. Steele went about the mop-up operation. He tidied the stump, bound it.

The rushes flickered out in anticlimax. Later, the production crew would tie up the program with interviews of the family, perhaps a shot of the funeral, a few observations on the problem of gangrene in the aged. Those things were the extras. What counted, what the viewers wanted, was the sheer nastiness of vicarious pain, and that they got in full measure. It was a gladiatorial contest without the gladiators, masochism concealed as medicine. It worked. It pulled in the viewers by the millions.

Northrop patted sweat from his forehead.

"Looks like we got ourselves quite a little show here, boys," he said in satisfaction.

The mood of satisfaction was still on him as he left the building that day. All day he had worked hard, getting the show into its final shape, cutting and polishing. He enjoyed the element of craftsmanship. It helped him to forget some of the sordidness of the program.

Night had fallen when he left. He stepped out of the main entrance and a figure strode forward, a bulky figure, medium height, tired face. A hand reached out, thrusting him roughly back into the lobby of the building.

At first Northrop didn't recognize the face of the man. It was a blank face, a nothing face, a middle-aged empty face. Then he placed it.

Harry Gardner. The son of the dead man.

"Murderer!" Gardner shrilled. "You killed him! He would have lived if you'd used anesthetics! You phony, you murdered him so people would have thrills on television!"

Northrop glanced up the lobby. Someone was coming, around the bend. Northrop felt calm. He could stare this nobody down until he fled in fear.

"Listen," Northrop said, "we did the best medical science can do for your father. We gave him the ultimate in scientific care. We—"

"You murdered him!"

"No," Northrop said, and then he said no more, because he saw the sudden flicker of a slice-gun in the blank-faced man's fat hand. He backed away, but it didn't help, because Gardner punched the trigger and an incandescent bolt flared out and sliced across Northrop's belly just as efficiently as the surgeon's scalpel had cut through the gangrenous leg.

Gardner raced away, feet clattering on the marble floor. Northrop dropped, clutching himself. His suit was seared, and there was a slash through his abdomen, a burn an eighth of an inch wide and perhaps four inches deep, cutting through intestines, through organs, through flesh. The pain hadn't begun yet. His nerves weren't getting the message through to his stunned brain. But then they were, and Northrop coiled and twisted in agony that was anything but vicarious now.

Footsteps approached.

"Jeez," a voice said.

Northrop forced an eye open. Maurillo. Of all people, Maurillo.

"A doctor," Northrop wheezed. "Fast! Christ, the pain! Help me, Ted!"

Maurillo looked down, and smiled. Without a word, he stepped to the telephone booth six feet away, dropped in a token, punched out a call.

"Get a van over here, fast. I've got a subject, Chief."

Northrop writhed in torment. Maurillo crouched next to him. "A doctor," Northrop murmured. "A needle, at least. Gimme a needle! The pain—"

"You want me to kill the pain?" Maurillo laughed. "Nothing doing, Chief. You just hang on. You stay alive till we get that hat on your head and tape the whole thing."

"But you don't work for me—you're off the program—"

"Sure," Maurillo said. "I'm with Transcontinental now.

They're starting a blood and guts show too. Only they don't need waivers."

Northrop gaped. Transcontinental? That bootleg outfit that peddled tapes in Afghanistan and Mexico and Ghana and God knew where else? Not even a network show, he thought. No fee. Dying in agony for the benefit of a bunch of lousy tapeleggers. That was the worst part, Northrop thought. Only Maurillo would pull a deal like that.

"A needle! For God's sake, Maurillo, a needle!"

"Nothing doing, Chief. The van'll be here any minute. They'll sew you up, and we'll tape it nice."

Northrop closed his eyes. He felt the coiling intestines blazing within him. He willed himself to die, to cheat Maurillo and his bunch of ghouls. But it was no use. He remained alive and suffering.

He lived for an hour. That was plenty of time to tape his dying agonies. The last thought he had was that it was a damned shame he couldn't star on his own show.

The Overlord's Thumb

The night before, the sun had gone down blood red, and Colonel John Devall had slept poorly because of it. The atmosphere on Markin was not normally conducive to blood-red sunsets, though they did happen occasionally on evenings when the blue of sunlight was scattered particularly well. The Marks connected red sunsets with approaching trouble. Colonel Devall, who headed the Terran cultural and military mission to Markin, was more cultural than military himself, and so he was willing to accept the Markin belief that the sunset was a premonition of conflict.

He was a tall man, well made and erect in bearing, with the sharp bright eyes and crisp manner of the military man. He successfully tried to project an appearance of authoritative officerhood, and his men respected and feared the image he showed them.

His degree was in anthropology. The military education was an afterthought, but a shrewd one; it had brought him command of the Markin outpost. The department of Extraterrestrial Affairs insisted that all missions to relatively primitive alien worlds be staffed and headed by military men—and, Devall reasoned, so long as I keep up the outward show, who's to know that I'm not the tough soldier they think I am? Markin was a peaceful enough world. The natives were intelligent, fairly highly advanced culturally if not technologically, easily dealt with on a rational being-to-being basis.

Which explains why Devall slept badly the night of the red sun. Despite his elegant posture and comportment, he regarded himself as essentially a bookish, unmilitary man. He had some doubts as to his own possible behavior in an unforeseen time of crisis. The false front of his officerhood might well crumble away under stress, and he knew it.

He dozed off finally, toward morning, having kicked the covers to the floor and twisted the sheet into crumpled confusion. It was a warmish night—most of them were, on Markin—but he felt chilled.

He woke late, only a few minutes before officers' mess, and dressed hurriedly in order to get there on time. As commanding officer, of course, he had the privilege of sleeping as late as he pleased—but getting up with the others was part of the mask Devall imposed on himself. He donned the light summer uniform, slapped depilator hastily on his tanned face, hooked on his formal blaster and belt, and signaled to his orderly that he was awake and ready.

The Terran enclave covered ten acres, half an hour's drive from one of the largest Markin villages. An idling jeep waited outside Devall's small private dome, and he climbed in, nodding curtly at the orderly.

"Morning, Harris."

"Good morning, sir. Sleep well?"

It was a ritual by now. "Very well," Devall responded automatically, as the jeep's turbos thrummed once and sent the little car humming across the compound to the mess hall. Clipped to the seat next to Devall was his daily morning program-sheet, prepared for him by the staffman-of-the-day while he slept. This morning's sheet was signed by Dudley, a major of formidable efficiency— Space Service through and through, a Military Wing career man and nothing else. Devall scanned the assignments for the morning, neatly written out in Dudley's crabbed hand.

Kelly, Dorfman, Mellors, Steber on Linguistic Detail, as usual. Same assignment as yesterday, in town.

Haskell on medic duty. Blood samples; urinalysis.

Matsuoko to maintenance staff (through Wednesday). Jolli on zoo detail.

Leonards, Meyer, Rodriguez on assigned botanical field trip, two days. Extra jeep assigned for specimen collection.

Devall scanned the rest of the list, but, as expected, Dudley had done a perfect job of deploying the men where they would be most useful and most happy. Devall thought briefly about Leonards, on the botanical field trip. A two-day trip might take him through the dangerous rain forest to the south; Devall felt a faint flicker of worry. The boy was his nephew, his sister's son—a reasonably competent journeyman botanist with the gold bar still untarnished on his shoulder. This was the boy's first commission; he had been assigned to Devall's unit at random, as a new man. Devall had concealed his relationship with Leonards from the other men, knowing it might make things awkward for the boy, but he still felt a protective urge.

Hell, the kid can take care of himself, Devall thought, and scribbled his initials at the bottom of the sheet and clipped it back in place; it would be posted now, while the men were cleaning their quarters and the officers ate, and by 0900 everyone would be out on his day's assignment. There was so much to do, Devall thought, and so little time to do it. There were so many worlds. . . .

He quitted the jeep and entered the mess hall. Officers' mess was a small well-lit alcove to the left of the main hall; as Devall entered he saw seven men standing stiffly at attention, waiting for him.

He knew they hadn't been standing that way all morning; they had snapped to attention only when their lookout—probably Second Lieutenant Leonards, the youngest—had warned them he was coming.

Well, he thought, it doesn't matter much. As long as appearance is preserved. The form.

"Good morning, gentlemen," he said crisply, and took his place at the head of the table.

For a while it looked as if it were going to turn out a pretty good day. The sun rose in a cloudless sky, and the thermometer tacked to the enclave flagstaff registered 93 degrees. When Markin got hot, it got *hot*. By noon, Devall knew by now, they could expect something like 110 in the shade—and then, a slow, steady decline into the low eighties by midnight.

The botanical crew departed on time, rumbling out of camp in two jeeps, and Devall stood for a moment on the mess hall steps watching them go, watching the other men head to their assigned posts. Stubble-faced Sergeant Jolli saluted him as he trotted across the compound to the zoo, where he would tend the little menagerie of Markin wildlife the expedition would bring back to Earth at termination. Wiry little Matsuoko passed by, dragging a carpenter's kit. The linguistic team climbed into its jeep and drove off toward town, where it would continue its studies in the Markin tongue.

They were all busy. The expedition had been on Markin just four months; eight months were left of their time. Unless an extension of stay came through, they'd pack up and return to Earth for six months of furlough-cum-report-session, and then it would be on to some other world for another year of residence.

Devall was not looking forward to leaving Markin. It was a pleasant world, if a little on the hot side, and there was no way of knowing what the *next* world would be like. A frigid ball of frozen methane, perhaps, where they would spend their year bundled into Valdez breathing-suits and trying to make contact with some species of intelligent ammonia-breathing mollusks. Better the devil we know, Devall felt.

But he had to keep moving on. This was his eleventh world, and there would be more to come. Earth had barely enough qualified survey teams to cover ten thousand worlds half-adequately, and life abounded on ten *million*. He would retain whichever members of the current team satisfied him by their performance, replace those who didn't fit in, and would go off to his next job.

He turned on the office fan and took down the logbook; unfastening the binder, he slipped the first blank sheet into the autotype. For once he avoided his standard blunder; he cleared his throat *before* switching on the autotype, thereby sparing the machine its customary difficulties in finding a verbal equivalent for his *Brghhumph!*

The guidelight glowed a soft red. Devall said, "Fourth April, two-seven-ought-five. Colonel John F. Devall recording. One hundred nineteenth day of our stay on Markin, World 7 of System 1106-sub-a.

"Temperature, 93 at 0900; wind gentle, southerly—"

He went on at considerable length, as he did each morning. Finishing off the required details, he gathered up the sheaf of specialty-reports that had been left at his door the night before, and began to read abstracts into the log; the autotype clattered merrily, and a machine somewhere in the basement of the towering E-T Affairs Building in Rio de Janeiro was reproducing his words as the subradio hookup transmitted them.

It was dull work; Devall often wondered whether he might have been ultimately happier doing simple anthropological field work, as he had once done, instead of taking on the onerous burden of routine that an administrative post entailed. *But someone has to shoulder the burden,* he thought.

Earthman's burden. We're the most advanced race; we help the others. But no one twists our arms to come out to these worlds and share what we have. Call it an inner compulsion.

He intended to work until noon; in the afternoon a Markin high priest was coming to the enclave to see him, and the interview would probably take almost till sundown. But about 1100 he was interrupted suddenly by the sound of jeeps unexpectedly entering the compound, and he heard the clamor of voices—both Terran voices and alien ones.

A fearful argument seemed to be in progress, but the group was too far away and Devall's knowledge of Markin too uncertain for him to be able to tell what was causing the rumpus. In some annoyance he snapped off the autotype, rose from his chair, and peered out the window into the yard.

Two jeeps had drawn up—the botanical crew, gone less than two hours. Four natives surrounded the three Earthmen. Two of the natives clutched barbed spears; a third was a woman, the fourth an old man. They were all protesting hotly over something.

Devall scowled; from the pale, tense, unhappy faces of the men in the jeep, he could tell something was very wrong. That blood-red sunset had foretold accurately, he thought as he dashed down the steps from his study.

Seven pairs of eyes focused on him as he strode toward the group: eight glittering alien eyes, warmly golden, and six shifting, uneasy Terran eyes.

"What's going on out here?" Devall demanded.

The aliens set up an immediate babble of noise, chattering away like a quartet of squirrels. Devall had never seen any of them behaving this way before.

"*Quiet!*" he roared.

In the silence that followed he said very softly, "Lieutenant Leonards, can you tell me exactly what all this fuss is about?"

The boy looked very frightened; his jaws were stiffly clenched, his lips bloodless. "Y-yes, sir," he said stammeringly. "Begging your pardon, sir. I seem to have killed an alien."

In the relative privacy of his office, Devall faced them all again—Leonards, sitting very quietly staring at his gleaming boots, Meyer and Rodriguez, who had accompanied him on the ill-starred botanizing journey. The aliens were outside; there was time to calm them down later.

"Okay," Devall said. "Leonards, I want you to repeat the story, exactly as you just told it to me, and I'll get it down on the autotype. Start talking when I point to you."

He switched on the autotype and said, "Testimony of Second Lieutenant Paul Leonards, Botanist, delivered in presence of commanding officer on 4 April 2705." He jabbed a forefinger at Leonards.

The boy's face looked waxy; beads of sweat dotted his pale vein-traced forehead, and his blond hair was tangled and twisted. He clamped his lips together in an agonized grimace, scratched the back of one hand, and finally said, "Well, we left the enclave about 0900 this morning, bound south and westerly on a tour of the outlying regions. Our purpose was to collect botanical specimens. I—was in charge of the group, which also included Sergeants Meyer and Rodriguez."

He paused. "We—we accomplished little in the first half hour; this immediate area had already been thoroughly covered by us anyway. But about 0945 Meyer noticed a heavily wooded area not far to the left of the main road, and called it to my attention. I suggested we stop and investigate. It was impossible to penetrate the wooded area in our jeeps, so we proceeded on foot. I left Rodriguez to keep watch over our gear while we were gone.

"We made our way through a close-packed stand of deciduous angiosperm trees of a species we had already studied, and found ourselves in a secluded area of natural growth, including several species which we could see were previously uncatalogued. We found one in particular—a shrub consisting of a single thick, succulent green stalk perhaps four feet high, topped by a huge gold-and-green composite flower head. We filmed it in detail, took scent samples, pollen prints, and removed several leaves."

Devall broke in suddenly. "You didn't pick the flower itself? Devall speaking."

"Of course not. It was the only specimen in the vicinity, and it's not our practice to destroy single specimens for the sake of collecting. But I did remove several leaves from the stalk. And the moment I did that, a native sprang at me from behind a thick clump of ferns.

"He was armed with one of those notched spears. Meyer saw him first and yelled, and I jumped back just as the alien came charging forward with his spear. I managed to deflect the spear with the outside of my arm and was not hurt. The alien fell back a few feet and shouted something at me in his language, which I don't understand too well as yet. Then he raised his spear and menaced me with it. I was carrying the standard-issue radial blaster. I drew it and ordered him in his own language to lower his spear, that we meant no harm. He ignored me and charged a second time. I fired in self-defense, trying to destroy the spear or at worst wound his arm, but he spun around to take the full force of the charge, and died instantly." Leonards shrugged. "That's about it, sir. We came back here at once."

"Umm. Devall speaking. Sergeant Meyer, would you say this account is substantially true?"

Meyer was a thin-faced, dark-haired man who was usually smiling, but he wasn't smiling now. "This is Sergeant Meyer. I'd say that Lieutenant Leonards told the story substantially as it occurred. Except that the alien didn't seem overly fierce despite his actions, in my opinion. I myself thought he was bluffing both times he charged, and I was a little surprised when Lieutenant Leonards shot him. That's all, sir."

Frowning, the Colonel said, "Devall speaking. This has been testimony in the matter of the alien killed by Lieutenant Leonards." He snapped off the autotype, stood up, and leaned forward across the desk, staring sternly at the trio of young botanists facing him.

"Sergeant Rodriguez, since you weren't present at the actual incident I'll consider you relieved of all responsibility in this matter, and your testimony won't be required. Report to Major Dudley for reassignment for the remainder of the week."

"Thank you, sir." Rodriguez saluted, grinned gratefully, and was gone.

"As for you two, though," Devall said heavily, "you'll both have to be confined to base pending the outcome of the affair. I don't need to tell you how serious this can be, whether the killing was in self-defense or not. Plenty of peoples don't understand the concept of self-defense." He moistened his suddenly dry lips. "I don't anticipate too many complications growing out of this. But these are alien people on an alien world, and their behavior is never certain."

He glanced at Leonards. "Lieutenant, I'll have to ask for your own safety that you remain in your quarters until further notice."

"Yes, sir. Is this to be considered arrest?"

"Not yet," Devall said. "Meyer, attach yourself to the maintenance platoon for the remainder of the day. We'll probably need your testimony again before this business is finished. Dismissed, both of you."

When they were gone, Devall sank back limply in his web-foam chair and stared at his fingertips. His hands were quivering as if they had a life of their own.

John F. Devall, Ph.D. Anthropology Columbia '82, commissioned Space Service Military Wing '87, and now you're in trouble for the first time.

How are you going to handle it, Jack? he asked himself. *Can you prove that that silver eagle really belongs on your shoulder?*

He was sweating. He felt very tired. He shut his eyes for a moment, opened them, and said into the intercom, "Send in the Marks."

Five of them entered, made ceremonial bows, and ranged themselves nervously along the far wall as if they were firing-squad candidates. Accompanying them came Steber of the linguistics team, hastily recalled from town to serve as an interpreter for Devall. The Colonel's knowledge of Markin was sketchy; he wanted Steber around in case any fine points had to be dealt with in detail.

The Marks were humanoid in structure, simian in ancestry, which should have made them close kin to the Terrans in general physiological structure. They weren't. Their skin was a rough, coarse, pebble-grained affair, dark-toned, running to muddy browns and occasional deep purples. Their jaws had somehow acquired a reptilian hinge in the course of evolution, which left them practically chinless but capable of swallowing food in huge lumps that would strangle an Earthman. Their eyes, liquid gold in color, were set wide in their heads, allowing enormous peripheral vision; their noses were flat buttons, in some cases barely perceptible bumps above the nostrils.

Devall saw two younger men, obviously warriors; they had left their weapons outside, but their jaws jutted belligerently, and the darker of the pair had virtually dislocated his jaw in rage. The woman looked like all the Mark women, shapeless and weary behind her shabby cloak of furs. The remaining pair were priests, one old, one *very* old. It was this ancient to whom Devall addressed his first remarks.

"I'm sorry that our meeting this afternoon has to be one of sorrow. I had been looking forward to a pleasant talk. But it's not always possible to predict what lies ahead."

"Death lay ahead for him who was killed," the old priest said in the dry, high-pitched tone of voice that Devall knew implied anger and scorn.

The woman let out a sudden wild ululation, half a dozen wailing words jammed together so rapidly Devall could not translate them. "What did she say?" he asked Steber.

The interpreter flattened his palms together thoughtfully. "She's the woman of the man who was killed. She was—demanding revenge," he said in English.

Apparently the two young warriors were friends of the dead man. Devall's eyes scanned the five hostile alien faces. "This is a highly regrettable incident," he said in Markin. "But I trust it won't affect the warm relationship between Earthman and Markin that has prevailed so far. This misunderstanding—"

"Blood must be atoned," said the smaller and less im-

pressively garbed of the two priests. He was probably the
local priest, Devall thought, and he was probably happy
to have his superior on hand to back him up.

The Colonel flicked the sweat from his forehead. "The
young man who committed the act will certainly be disciplined. Of course you realize that a killing in self-
defense cannot be regarded as murder, but I admit the
young man did act unwisely and will suffer the consequences." It didn't sound too satisfying to Devall, and,
indeed, the aliens hardly seemed impressed.

The high priest uttered two short, sharp syllables. They
were not words in Devall's vocabulary, and he looked over
at Steber in appeal.

"He said Leonards was trespassing on sacred ground.
He said the crime they're angry about is not murder but
blasphemy."

Despite the heat, Devall felt a sudden chill. *Not . . .
murder? This is going to be complicated,* he realized
gloomily.

To the priest he said, "Does this change the essential
nature of the case? He'll still be punished by us for his
action, which can't be condoned."

"You may punish him for murder, if you so choose,"
the high priest said, speaking very slowly, so Devall
would understand each word. The widow emitted some
highly terrestrial-sounding sobs; the young men glowered
stolidly. "Murder is not our concern," the high priest
went on. "He has taken life; life belongs to Them, and
They withdraw it whenever They see fit, by whatever
means They care to employ. But he has also desecrated a
sacred flower on sacred ground. These are serious crimes,
to us. Added to this he has shed the blood of a Guardian,
on sacred ground. We ask you to turn him over to us for
trial by a priestly court on this double charge of blasphemy. Afterward, perhaps, you may try him by your

own laws, for whichever one of them he has broken."

For an instant all Devall saw was the old priest's implacable leathery face; then he turned and caught the expression of white-faced astonishment and dismay Steber displayed.

It took several seconds for the high priest's words to sink in, and several more before Devall came to stunned realization of the implications. *They want to try an Earthman,* he thought numbly. *By their own law. In their own court. And mete out their own punishment.*

This had abruptly ceased being a mere local incident, an affair to clean up, note in the log, and forget. It was no longer a matter of simple reparations for the accidental killing of an alien.

Now, thought Devall dully, it was a matter of galactic importance. And he was the man who had to make all the decisions.

He visited Leonards that evening, after the meal. By that time everyone in the camp knew what had happened, though Devall had ordered Steber to keep quiet about the alien demand to try Leonards themselves.

The boy looked up as Devall entered his room, and managed a soggy salute.

"At ease, Lieutenant." Devall sat on the edge of Leonards' bed and squinted up at him. "Son, you're in very hot water now."

"Sir, I—"

"I know. You didn't mean to pluck leaves off the sacred bramble-bush, and you couldn't help shooting down the native who attacked you. And if this business were as simple as all that, I'd reprimand you for hotheadedness and let it go at that. But—"

"But what, sir?"

Devall scowled and forced himself to face the boy squarely.

"But the aliens want to try you themselves. They aren't so much concerned with the murder as they are with your double act of blasphemy. That withered old high priest wants to take you before an ecclesiastical court."

"You won't allow *that,* of course, will you, Colonel?" Leonards seemed confident that such an unthinkable thing could never happen.

"I'm not so sure, Paul," Devall said quietly, deliberately using the boy's first name.

"*What,* sir?"

"This is evidently something very serious you've committed. That high priest is calling a priestly convocation to deal with you. They'll be back here to get you tomorrow at noon, he said."

"But you wouldn't turn me over to them, sir! After all, I was on duty; I had no knowledge of the offense I was committing. Why, it's none of their business!"

"Make *them* see that," Devall said flatly. "They're aliens. They don't understand Terran legal codes. They don't *want* to hear about our laws; by *theirs,* you've blasphemed, and blasphemers must be punished. This is a law-abiding race on Markin. They're an ethically advanced society, regardless of the fact that they're not technologically advanced. Ethically they're on the same plane we are."

Leonards looked terribly pale. "You'll turn me over to them?"

Devall shrugged. "I didn't say that. But look at it from my position. I'm leader of a cultural and military mission. Our purpose is to live among these people, learn their ways, guide them as much as we can in our limited time here. We at least *try* to make a pretense of respecting their rights as individuals and as a species, you know.

"Well, now it's squarely on the line. Are we friends living among them and helping them, or are we overlords grinding them under our thumbs?"

"Sir, I'd say that was an oversimplification," Leonards remarked hesitantly.

"Maybe so. But the issue's clear enough. If we turn them down, it means we're setting up a gulf of superiority between Earth and these aliens, despite the big show we made about being brothers. And word will spread to other planets. We try to sound like friends, but our actions in the celebrated Leonards case reveal our true colors. We're arrogant, imperialistic, patronizing, and —well, do you see?"

"So you're going to turn me over to them for trial, then," the boy said quietly.

Devall shook his head. "I don't know. I haven't made up my mind yet. If I turn you over, it'll certainly set a dangerous precedent. And if I don't—I'm not sure what will happen." He shrugged. "I'm going to refer the case back to Earth. It isn't my decision to make."

But it *was* his decision to make, he thought, as he left the boy's quarters and headed stiff-legged toward the Communications shack. He was on the spot, and only he could judge the complex factors that controlled the case. Earth would almost certainly pass the buck back to him.

He was grateful for one thing, though: at least Leonards hadn't made an appeal to him on family grounds. That was cause for pride, and some relief. The fact that the boy was his nephew was something he'd have to blot rigorously from his mind until all this was over.

The signalman was busy in the back of the shack, bent over a crowded worktable. Devall waited a moment, cleared his throat gently, and said, "Mr. Rory?"

Rory turned. "Yes, Colonel?"

"Put through a subradio to Earth for me, immediately. To Director Thornton at the E-T Department. And yell for me when you've made contact."

It took twenty minutes for the subspace impulse to leap out across the light-years and find a receiver on Earth, ten minutes more for it to pass through the relay point and on to Rio. Devall returned to the shack to find the lambent green solido field in tune and waiting for him. He stepped through and discovered himself standing a few feet before the desk of the E-T Department's head. Thornton's image was sharp, but the desk seemed to waver at the edges. Solid non-organic objects always came through poorly.

Quickly Devall reviewed the situation. Thornton sat patiently, unmoving, till the end of it; hands knotted rigidly, lean face set, he might have been a statue. Finally he commented, "Unpleasant business."

"Quite."

"The alien is returning the next day, you say? I'm afraid that doesn't give us much time to hold a staff meeting and explore the problem, Colonel Devall."

"I could probably delay him a few days."

Thornton's thin lips formed a tight bloodless line. After an instant he said, "No. Take whatever action you deem necessary, Colonel. If the psychological pattern of the race is such that unfortunate consequences would result if you refused to allow them to try your man, then you must certainly turn him over. If the step can be avoided, of course, avoid it. The man must be punished in any case."

The Director smiled bleakly. "You're one of our best

men, Colonel. I'm confident you'll arrive at an ultimately satisfactory resolution to this incident."

"Thank you, sir," Devall said, in a dry, uncertain voice.
He nodded and stepped back out of field range. Thornton's image seemed to flicker; Devall caught one last dis-
missing sentence, "Report back to me when the matter is
settled," and then the field died.

He stood alone in the shabby Communications shack,
blinking in the sudden darkness that rolled in over him
after the solidophone's intense light, and after a moment
began to pick his way over the heaps of equipment and
out into the compound.

It was as he had expected. Thornton was a good man,
but he was a civilian appointee, subject to government
control. He disliked making top-level decisions—particularly when a Colonel a few hundred light-years away
could be forced into making them for him.

Devall called a meeting of his top staff men for 0915
the following morning. Work at the base had been all but
suspended; the linguistics team was confined to the area,
and Devall had ordered guards posted at all exits. Vio-
lence could rise unexpectedly among even the most placid
of alien peoples; it was impossible to predict the moment
when a racial circuit-breaker would cease to function and
fierce hatred burst forth.

They listened in silence to the tapes of Leonards'
statements, Meyer's comments, and the brief interview
Devall had had with the five aliens. Devall punched the
cutoff stud and glanced rapidly around the table at his
men: two majors, a captain, and a quartet of lieutenants comprised his high staff, and one of the lieutenants
was confined to quarters.

"That's the picture. The old high priest is showing up

here about noon for my answer. I thought I'd toss the thing open for staff discussion first."

Major Dudley asked for the floor.

He was a short, stocky man with dark flashing eyes, and on several occasions in the past had been known to disagree violently with Devall on matters of procedure. Devall had picked him for four successive trips, despite this; the Colonel believed in diversity of opinion, and Dudley was a tremendously efficient organizer as well.

"Major?"

"Sir, it doesn't seem to me that there's any question of what action to take. It's impossible to hand Leonards over to them for trial. It's—inhuman, or—un-Earthlike!"

Devall frowned. "Would you elaborate, Major?"

"Simple enough. We're the race who developed the space-drive—therefore, we're the galaxy's most advanced race. I think that goes without saying."

"It does not," Devall commented. "But go ahead."

Scowling, Dudley said, "Regardless of your opinion, *sir*—the aliens we've encountered so far have all regarded us as their obvious superiors. I don't think that can be denied—and I think it can only be attributed to the fact that we *are* their superiors. Well, if we give up Leonards for trial, it cheapens our position. It makes us look weak, spineless. We—"

"You're suggesting, then," Devall broke in, "that we hold the position of overlords in the galaxy—and by yielding to our serfs, we may lose all control over them. Is this your belief, Major?" Devall glared at him.

Dudley met the Colonel's angry gaze calmly. "Basically, yes. Dammit, sir, I've tried to make you see this ever since the Hegath expedition. We're not out here in the stars to collect butterflies and squirrels! We—"

"Out of order," Devall snapped coldly. "This is a cultural mission as well as a military one, Major—and so long as I'm in command it remains primarily cultural." He felt on the verge of losing his temper. He glanced away from Dudley and said, "Major Grey, could I hear from you?"

Grey was the ship's astrogator; on land his functions were to supervise stockade construction and mapmaking. He was a wiry, unsmiling little man with razorlike cheekbones and ruddy skin. "I feel we have to be cautious, sir. Handing Leonards over would result in a tremendous loss of Terran prestige."

"*Loss?*" Dudley burst in. "It would cripple us! We'd never be able to hold our heads up honestly in the galaxy again if—"

Calmly Devall said, "Major Dudley, you've been ruled out of order. Leave this meeting, Major. I'll discuss a downward revision of your status with you later." Turning back to Grey without a further glance at Dudley, he said, "You don't believe, Major, that such an action would have a correspondingly *favorable* effect on our prestige in the eyes of those worlds inclined to regard Earth uneasily?"

"That's an extremely difficult thing to determine in advance, sir."

"Very well, then." Devall rose. "Pursuant to regulations, I've brought this matter to the attention of authorities on Earth, and have also offered it for open discussion among my officers. Thanks for your time, gentlemen."

Captain Marechal said uncertainly. "Sir, won't there be any vote on our intended course of action?"

Devall grinned coldly. "As commanding officer of this base, I'll take the sole responsibility upon myself for the decision in this particular matter. It may make things easier for all of us in the consequent event of a court-martial inquiry."

It was the only way, he thought, as he waited tensely in his office for the high priest to arrive. The officers seemed firmly set against any conciliatory action, in the name of Terra's prestige. It was hardly fair for him to make them take responsibility for a decision that might be repugnant to them.

Too bad about Dudley, Devall mused. But insubordination of that sort was insufferable; Dudley would have to be dropped from the unit on their next trip out. If there is any next trip out for me, he added.

The intercom glowed gently. "Yes?"

"Alien delegation is here, sir," said the orderly.

"Don't send them in until I signal."

He strode to the window and looked out. The compound, at first glance, seemed full of aliens. Actually there were only a dozen, he realized, but they were clad in full panoply, bright red and harsh green robes, carrying spears and ornamental swords. Half a dozen enlisted men were watching them nervously from a distance, their hands ready to fly to blasters instantly if necessary.

He weighed the choices one last time.

If he handed Leonards over, the temporary anger of the aliens would be appeased—but perhaps at a long-range cost to Earth's prestige. Devall had long regarded himself as an essentially weak man with a superb instinct for camouflage—but would his yielding to the aliens imply to the universe that all Earth was weak?

On the other hand, he thought, suppose he refused to release Leonards to the aliens. Then, he would be, in essence, bringing down the overlord's thumb, letting the universe know that Earthmen were responsible only to themselves and not to the peoples of the worlds they visited.

Either way, he realized, the standing of Earthmen in the galaxy's estimation would suffer. One way, they would look like appeasing weaklings; the other, like tyrants. He remembered a definition he had once read: *melodrama is the conflict of right and wrong, tragedy the conflict of right and right.* Both sides were right here. Whichever way he turned, there would be difficulties.

And there was an additional factor: the boy. What if they executed him? Family considerations seemed absurdly picayune at this moment, but still, to hand his own nephew over for possible execution at the hands of an alien people—

He took a deep breath, straightened his shoulders, sharpened the hard gaze of his eyes. A glance at the mirror over the bookcase told him he looked every inch the commanding officer; not a hint of the inner conflict showed through.

He depressed the intercom stud. "Send in the high priest. Let the rest of them wait outside."

The priest looked impossibly tiny and wrinkled, a gnome of a man whose skin was fantastically gullied and mazed by extreme age. He wore a green turban over his hairless head—a mark of deep mourning, Devall knew.

The little alien bowed low, extending his pipestem arms behind his back at a sharp angle, indicating respect. When he straightened, his head craned back sharply, his small round eyes peering directly into Devall's.

"The jury has been selected; the trial is ready to begin. Where is the boy?"

Devall wished fleetingly he could have had the services of an interpreter for this last interview. But that was impossible; this was something he had to face alone, without help.

"The accused man is in his quarters," Devall said slowly. "First I want to ask some questions, old one."

"Ask."

"If I give you the boy to try, will there be any chance of his receiving the death penalty?"

"It is conceivable."

Devall scowled. "Can't you be a little more definite than that?"

"How can we know the verdict before the trial takes place?"

"Let that pass," Devall said, seeing he would get no concrete reply. "Where would you try him?"

"Not far from here."

"Could I be present at the trial?"

"No."

Devall had learned enough of Markin grammar by now to realize that the form of the negative the priest had employed meant literally, I-say-*no*-and-mean-what-I-say. Moistening his lips, he said, "Suppose I should refuse to turn Lieutenant Leonards over to you for trial? How could I expect your people to react?"

There was a long silence. Finally the old priest said, "Would you do such a thing?"

"I'm speaking hypothetically." (Literally, the form was, I-speak-on-a-cloud.)

"It would be very bad. We would be unable to purify the sacred garden for many months. Also—" he added a sentence of unfamiliar words. Devall puzzled unsuccessfully over their meaning for nearly a minute.

"What does that mean?" he asked at length. "Phrase it in different words."

"It is the name of a ritual. I would have to stand trial in the Earthman's place—and I would die," the priest said simply. "Then my successor would ask you all to go away."

The office seemed very quiet; the only sounds Devall heard were the harsh breathing of the old priest and the off-key chirruping of the cricketlike insects that infested the grassplot outside the window.

Appeasement? he wondered. *Or the overlord's thumb*?

Suddenly there seemed no doubt at all in his mind of what he should do, and he wondered how he could have hesitated indecisively so long.

"I hear and respect your wishes, old one," he said, in a ritual formula of renunciation Steber had taught him. "The boy is yours. But can I ask a favor?"

"Ask."

"He didn't know he was offending your laws. He meant well; he's sincerely sorry for what he did. He's in your hands, now—but I want to ask mercy on his behalf. He had no way of knowing he was offending."

"This will be seen at the trial," the old priest said coldly. "If there is to be mercy, mercy will be shown him. I make no promises."

"Very well," Devall said. He reached for a pad and scrawled an order remanding Lieutenant Paul Leonards to the aliens for trial, and signed it with his full name and title. "Here. Give this to the Earthman who let you in. He'll see to it that the boy is turned over to you."

"You are wise," the priest said. He bowed elaborately and made for the door.

"Just one moment," Devall said desperately, as the alien opened the door. "Another question."

"Ask," the priest said.

"You told me you'd take his place if I refused to let you have him. Well, how about another substitute? Suppose—"

"*You* are not acceptable to us," the priest said as if reading Devall's mind, and left.

Five minutes later the Colonel glanced out his window and saw the solemn procession of aliens passing through the exit-posts and out of the compound. In their midst, unprotesting, was Leonards. He didn't look back, and Devall was glad of it.

The Colonel stared at the row of books a long time, the frayed spools that had followed him around from world to world, from gray Danelon to stormy Lurrin to bone-dry Korvel, and on to Hegath and M'Qualt and the others, and now to warm, blue-skied Markin. Shaking his head, he turned away and dropped heavily into the foam cradle behind his desk.

He snapped on the autotype with a savage gesture and dictated a full account of his actions, from the very start until his climactic decision, and smiled bitterly; there would be a certain time-lag, but before long the autotype facsimile machine in the E-T Department's basement would start clacking, there in Rio, and Thornton would know what Devall had done.

And Thornton would be stuck with it as Department policy henceforth.

Devall switched on the intercom and said, "I'm not to be disturbed under any circumstances. If there's anything urgent, have it sent to Major Grey; he's acting head of the base until I countermand. And if any messages come from Earth, let Grey have them, too."

He wondered if they'd relieve him of his command immediately, or wait until he got back to Earth. The latter, more likely; Thornton had some subtlety, if not much. But there was certain to be an inquiry, and someone's head would have to roll.

Devall shrugged and stretched back. *I did what was right*, he told himself firmly. *That's the one thing I can be sure of.*

But I hope I don't ever have to face my sister again.

He dozed, after a while, eyes half open and slipping rapidly closed. Sleep came to him, and he welcomed it, for he was terribly tired.

He was awakened suddenly by a loud outcry. A jubilant shout from a dozen throats at once, splitting the afternoon calm. Devall felt a moment's disorientation; then, awakening rapidly, he sprang to the window and peered out.

A figure—alone and on foot—was coming through the open gateway. He wore regulation uniform, but it was dripping wet and torn in several places. His blond hair was plastered to his scalp as if he had been swimming; he looked fatigued.

Leonards.

The Colonel was nearly halfway out the front door before he realized that his uniform was in improper order. He forced himself back, tidied his clothing, and with steely dignity strode out the door a second time.

Leonards stood surrounded by a smiling knot of men, enlisted men and officers alike. The boy was grinning wearily.

"Attention!" Devall barked, and immediately the area fell silent. He stepped forward.

Leonards raised one arm in an exhausted salute. There were some ugly bruises on him, Devall noticed.

"I'm back, Colonel."

"I'm aware of that. You understand that I'll have to return you to the Marks for trial anyway, despite your no doubt daring escape?"

The boy smiled and shook his head. "No, sir. You don't follow, sir. The trial's over. I've been tried and acquitted."

"What's that?"

"It was trial by ordeal, Colonel. They prayed for half an hour or so, and then they dumped me in the lake down the road. The dead man's two brothers came after me and tried to drown me, but I outswam them and came up safely on the other side."

He shook his hair like a drenched cat, scattering a spray of water several feet in the air. "They nearly had me, once. But as soon as I got across the lake alive and undrowned, it proved to them I couldn't have meant any harm. So they declared me innocent, apologized, and turned me loose. They were still praying when I left them."

There seemed to be no bitterness in Leonards' attitude; apparently, Devall thought, he had understood the reason for the decision to hand him over and would not hold it against him now. That was gratifying.

"You'd better get to your quarters and dry off, Lieutenant. And then come to my office. I'd like to talk to you there."

"Yes, sir."

Devall spun sharply and headed back across the clearing to his office. He slammed the door behind him and switched on the autotype. The report to Earth would have to be amended now.

A moment or two after he had finished, the intercom glowed. He turned it on and heard Steber's voice saying, "Sir, the old priest is here. He wants to apologize to you for everything. He's wearing clothing of celebration, and he brought a peace offering for us."

"Tell him I'll be right out," Devall said, "and call all the men together. Including Dudley. *Especially* Dudley. I want him to see this."

He slipped off his sweat-stained jacket and took a new one out. Surveying himself in the mirror, he nodded approvingly.

Well, well, he thought. *So the boy came through it safely. That's good.*

But he knew that the fate of Paul Leonards had been irrelevant all along, except on the sheerly personal level. It was the larger issue that counted.

For the first time, Earth had made a concrete demonstration of the equality-of-intelligent-life doctrine it had been preaching so long. He had shown that he respected the Markin laws in terms of what they were *to the Marks,* and he had won the affection of a race as a result. Having the boy return unharmed was in the nature of an unbegged bonus.

But the precedent had been set. And the next time, perhaps, on some other world, the outcome might not be so pleasant. Some cultures had pretty nasty ways of putting criminals to death.

He realized that the burden the Earth exploration teams carried now had become many times heavier— that now, Earthmen would be subject to the laws of the planets who hosted them, and no more unwitting botanical excursions into sacred gardens could be tolerated. But it was for the ultimate good, he thought. We've shown them that we're not overlords, and that most of us don't want to be overlords. And now the thumb comes down on *us.*

He opened the door and stepped out. The men had gathered, and the old priest knelt abjectly at the foot of the steps, bearing some sort of enameled box as his offering. Devall smiled and returned the bow, and lifted the old alien gently to his feet.

We'll have to be on our best behavior from now on, he thought. *We'll really have to watch our steps. But it'll be worth it.*

The Outbreeders

The week before his impending marriage, Ryly Baille went alone into the wild forests that separated Baille lands from those of the Clingert clan. The lonely journey was a prenuptial tradition among the Bailles; his people expected him to return with body toughened by exertion, mind sharp and clear from solitary meditation. No one at all expected him to meet and fall in love with a Clingert girl.

He left early on a Threeday morning; nine Bailles saw him off. Old Fredrog, the Baille Clanfather, wished him well. Minton, Ryly's own father, clasped him by the hand for a long, awkward moment. Three of his patrilineal cousins offered their best wishes. And Davud, his dearest friend and closest phenotype-brother, slapped him affectionately.

Ryly said good-bye also to his mother, to the Clanmother, and to Hella, his betrothed. He shouldered his bow and quiver, hitched up his hiking trousers, and grinned nervously. Overhead, Thomas, the yellow primary sun, was rising high; later in the day the blue companion, Doris, would join her husband in the sky. It was a warm spring morning.

Ryly surveyed the little group: six tall, blond-haired, blue-eyed men, three tall, red-haired, hazel-eyed women. Perfect examples all of Baille-norm, and therefore the highest representatives of evolution.

"So long, all," he said smilingly. There was nothing

135

else to say. He turned and headed off into the chattering forest. His long legs carried him easily down the well-worn path. Tradition required him to follow the main path until noon, when the second sun would enter the sky; then, wherever he might be, he was to veer sharply from the road and hew his own way through the vegetation for the rest of the journey.

He would be gone three days, two nights. On the third evening he would turn back, returning by morning to claim his bride.

He thought of Hella as he walked. She was a fine girl; he was happy Clanfather had allotted her to him. Not that she was prettier than any of the other current eligibles, Ryly thought—they were all more or less equal, anyway. But Hella had a certain bright sparkle, a way of smiling, that Ryly thought he could grow to like.

Thomas was climbing now toward his noon height; the forest grew warm. A bright-colored web-winged lizard sprang squawking from a tree to the left of the path and fluttered in a brief clumsy arc over Ryly's head. He notched an arrow and brought the lizard down—his first kill of the trip. Tucking three red pinlike tail feathers in his belt, he moved on.

At noon the first blue rays of Doris mingled with the yellow of Thomas. The moment had come. Ryly knelt to mutter a short prayer in memory of those two pioneering Bailles who had come to The World so many generations ago to found the clan, and swung off to the right, cutting between the fuzzy gray boles of two towering sweetfruit trees. He incised his name on the forestward side of one tree, as a guide-sign for his return, and entered the unknown part of the forest.

He walked till he was hungry; then he killed an unwary bouncer, skinned, cooked, and ate the meaty rodent, and bathed in a crystal-bright stream at the edge of an evergreen thicket. When darkness came, he camped near an upjutting cliff, and for a long time lay on his back, staring up at the four gleaming little moons, telling himself the old clan legends until he fell asleep.

The following morning was without event; he covered many miles, carefully leaving trail-marks behind. And shortly before Dorisrise he met the girl.

It was really an accident. He had sighted the yellow dorsal spines of a wabbler protruding a couple of inches over the top of a thick hedge, and decided the wabbler's horns would be as good a trophy as any to bring back to Hella. He strung his bow and waited for the beast to lift its one vulnerable spot, the eye, into view.

After a moment the wabbler's head appeared, top-heavy with the weight of the spreading snout-horns. Ryly fingered his bowstring and targeted on the blood-shot eye.

His aim was false; the arrow thwacked hard against the scalelike black leather of the wabbler's domed skull, hung, penetrating the skin for an instant, and dropped away. The wabbler snorted in surprise and anger and set off, crashing noisily through the under-brush, undulating wildly as its vast flippers slammed the ground with each frantic step.

Ryly gave chase. He strung his bow on the run, as he followed the trail of the big herbivore. Somewhere ahead a waterfall rumbled; the wabbler evidently in-tended to make an aquatic getaway. Ryly broke into a clearing—and saw the girl standing next to the wabbler, patting its muscular withers and murmuring soothing sounds. She glared up at Ryly as he appeared.

For a moment he hardly recognized her as human. She was slim and dark-haired, with great black eyes, a tiny tilted nose, full pouting lips. She wore a brightly colored saronglike affair of some batik cloth; it left her tanned legs bare. And she was almost a foot shorter than Ryly; Baille women rarely dipped below five-ten in height.

"Did you shoot at this animal?" she demanded suddenly.

Ryly had difficulty understanding her; the words seemed to be in his language, but the vowels sounded all wrong, the consonants not harsh enough.

"I did," he said. "I didn't know he was your pet."

"*Pet!* The wabblers aren't pets. They're sacred. Are you a Baille?"

Taken aback by the abrupt question, Ryly sputtered a moment before nodding an affirmative.

"I thought so. I'm Joanne Clingert. What are you doing on Clingert territory?"

"So that's it," Ryly said slowly. He stared at her as if she had just crawled out from under a lichen-crusted rock. "You're a *Clingert.* That explains things."

"Explains what?"

"The way you look, the way you talk, the way you . . ." He moved hesitantly closer, looking down at her. She looked very angry, but behind the anger shone something else—

A sparkle, maybe. A brightness.

Ryly shuddered. The Clingerts were dreaded alien beings of a terrible ugliness, or so Clanfather had constantly reiterated. Well, maybe so. But, then, *this* Clingert could hardly be typical. She seemed so delicate and lovely, quite unlike the rawboned, athletic Baille women.

A blue shaft of light broke through the saw-toothed leaves of the trees and shattered on the Clingert's brow. Almost as a reflex, Ryly sank to his knees to pray.

"Why are you doing that?" the Clingert asked.

"It's Dorisrise! Don't you pray at Dorisrise?"

She glanced upward at the blue sun now orbiting the

yellow primary. "That's only Secundus that just rose. What did you call it—*Doris*?"

Ryly concluded his prayer and rose. "Of course. And there's Thomas next to her."

"Hmm. We call them Primus and Secundus. But I suppose it's not surprising that the Bailles and the Clingerts would have different names for the suns. Thomas and Doris . . . that's nice. Named for the original Bailles?"

Ryly nodded. "And I guess Primus and Secundus founded the Clingerts?"

She laughed—a brittle tinkling sound that bounced prettily back from the curtain of trees. "No, hardly. Jarl and Bess were our founders. Primus and Secundus only means First and Second, in Latin."

"Latin? What's that? I—"

Ryly shut his mouth, suddenly. A cold tremor of delayed alarm passed through him. He stared at the Clingert in horror.

"Is something wrong?" the Clingert asked. "You look so pale."

"We're talking to each other," Ryly said. "We're holding a nice little conversation. Very friendly, and all."

She looked indignant. "Is anything wrong with that?"

"Yes," Ryly said glumly. "I'm supposed to hate you."

They walked together to the place where the waterfall cascaded in a bright foaming tumble down the mountainside, and they talked. And Ryly discovered that Clingerts were not quite so frightening as he had been led to believe.

His wanderings had brought him close to Clingert territory; Joanne had been but an hour from home when she had met him. But he nervously declined an offer to come to the Clingert settlement with her. That would be carrying things much too far.

After a while the Clingert said, "Do you hate me yet?"

"I don't think I'm going to hate you," Ryly told her. "I think I like you. And particularly every time I think of Hella—"

"Hella?" The Clingert's eyes flashed angrily.

"The Baille who was my betrothed." He accented the *was*. "Clanfather gave her to me last month. We were supposed to be married when I returned to the settlement. I thought I was looking forward to it too. Until—until—"

A wabbler mooed somewhere deeper in the forest. Ryly stared helplessly at the Clingert, realizing now what was happening to him.

He was falling in love with the Clingert.

Ever since the days when Thomas and Doris Baille first came to The World, Baille and Clingert had kept firm boundaries. Baille had mated only with Baille. And now—

Ryly shook his head sadly. In the blue-and-gold brilliance of the afternoon, this Clingert seemed infinitely more desirable to him than any Baille woman ever had.

She touched his hand gently. "You're very quiet. You're not at all like the Clingert men."

"I guess I'm not. What are they like?"

She made a little face. "Much shorter than you are, with ugly straight dark hair and black eyes. Their muscles bunch up in knots when they draw bows; your arms are long and lean. And Clingert men get bald at a very young age." Her hand lightly ruffled his Baille-yellow hair. "Do Bailles lose their hair young?"

"Bailles never get bald. Clanfather's hair is still as yellow as mine, and he's past fifty." Ryly fell silent again, thinking of Clanfather and what he would say if he knew what had taken place out here.

Not since the days when Thomas cast the first Clingert

from his sight has this happened, he would probably intone in a deep, sententious voice.

Ryly remembered a time far away in his childhood when a Baille woman had birthed a dark-haired son. Clanfather had driven child and parents out into the forest, and there other Bailles had stoned them. Ryly was not anxious to share that fate. But yet—

He scrambled to his feet. The Clingert looked at him in alarm. "Where are you going?" she asked.

"Back. To the Baille settlement."

There was a moment of silence between them. Finally Ryly took a deep breath and said, "I'll return. Meet me at this place three days from now, at Dorisrise—I mean, when Secundus rises. Will you be here?"

Uneasiness glimmered in her dark eyes. "Yes," she said.

He reached the familiar Baille territory near nightfall the next day, having covered the outlying ground as rapidly as he could and with as few stops along the way as possible. He ducked back onto the main road around the time of Thomasset on Fiveday. He had had little difficulty in locating the tree that bore his name in its bark. Only the blue sun shone now, and it was low above the horizon; the moons were beginning their procession across the twilight-dimmed sky.

Ryly stole into the settlement on the back road. That route brought him past the crude little cabin which Thomas had built with his own hands as a place for Doris and himself to live, long ago when the first Bailles had tumbled out of the sky and settled on The World. Ryly quivered a little as he passed the dingy old shrine; the sort of betrayal he was contemplating did not come easy to him.

Above all, he did not want to be seen. Not until he had spoken with his phenotype-brother Davud.

A cat mewled. Ryly ducked into the concealing darkness of a vine bower and waited. A stiff-necked old man passed by: Clanfather. Ryly held his breath until the old one had entered the Clan house; he slipped out of his shelter then, padded silently across the main courtyard, and ran into the open archway that led to Davud's cabin.

The light was on. Davud was inside, drowsing in a chair. Ryly tiptoed through the rear door. He sprang across the room in four big bounds and clapped his hands over Davud's mouth before the other had fully come awake.

"It's me—Ryly. I'm back."

"*Mmph!*"

"Keep quiet and don't make any loud noises. I don't want people to find out I'm here yet."

He stepped back. Davud rubbed his lips and said, "What in Thomas' name made you want to scare me like that? For a second I thought it was a Clingert raid."

Ryly winced. He stared intently at Davud, wondering if it was safe to tell him. Davud, of all the Bailles, was closest to him in physique and in attitudes, which was the reason Clanfather had designated them phenotype-brothers even though they had different parents. Among the Bailles, actual parentage meant little, since genetically every clan member was virtually identical to every other.

He and Davud were uncannily alike, though: both standing six-three, the Baille-norm height, both with the same twist to their unruly blond hair, the same sharpness of nose, and the same thinness of earlobe. Ryly hoped Davud's mental makeup now was similar as well.

He poured a beaker of thick yellow bryophyte wine and sipped it slowly to steady his nerves. "I have to talk to you, Davud. Something very important has happened to me."

Ignoring that, Davud said, "You weren't supposed to come back until tomorrow morning. I saw Hella around

Thomasset, and she said she couldn't wait to see you again." Davud grinned. "I told her I was enough like you to do, but she wouldn't listen to the idea."

"Don't talk about Hella. Listen to me, Davud. I went into Clingert territory on my trip. I met a Clingert girl. I . . . love her . . . I think."

Davud was on his feet in an instant, facing Ryly, brow to brow, chin to chin. His nostrils were quivering. "What did you just say?"

Very quietly Ryly repeated his words.

"I thought that was it," Davud muttered. "Ryly, are you out of your head? Marry a Clingert? That *filth*?"

"But you haven't seen—"

"I don't need to see. You know the old stories of how the first Clingert quarreled with Thomas until Thomas was forced to drive him away. You know what sort of creatures the Clingerts are. How can you possibly—"

"Love one? Davud, you don't know how easy it is. The Baille girls are so damned big and brawny! Joanne is— well, you'd have to see her to know. The fact that Thomas and the first Clingert had some silly quarrel hundreds of years ago—"

Davud's face was a white mask of indignation. "*Ryly!* Get hold of yourself! You're talking nonsense, man— absolute nonsense. Baille and Clingert must never breed. Would you want to pollute our line with theirs?"

"Yes." Defiantly.

"You're mad, then. But why did you come back here to tell me about all this? Why didn't you simply stay with your Clingert?"

"I wanted someone to know. Someone I could trust— like you."

"You made a mistake in that case," Davud said. "I'm going to tell Clanfather the whole story, and when they stone you I'll be glad to take part. That's what they did the last time this happened, fifteen years ago, if you remember. When Luri Baille had a baby that looked like a Clingert. The line has to be kept pure."

"Why?"

"It—it has to, that's all," Davud said weakly. As Ryly started to walk out, he added, "Hey! Where do you think you're going?"

"Back to the forest," Ryly said in a bitter voice. "I promised her I'd be back. I should never have come here in the first place." He was shaking and perspiring heavily; somewhat to his own surprise he realized that by this conversation he had effectively cut himself off from the Bailles forever.

"You're not going, Ryly. I won't let you."

Davud grabbed Ryly's collar, but he pulled away. "Don't try to stop me, Davud."

Without replying, Davud gripped the fleshy part of his arm. Calmly Ryly pivoted and smashed his fist into the face that was so much like his own. Davud blinked, half believing, and started to mutter something. Ryly quickly jerked his arm free and hit Davud a second time. Davud sagged to the floor.

Ryly stood poised indecisively for a second, watching with some astonishment the flow of blood from his phenotype-brother's broken nose. Then he turned and dashed through the doorway, out into the dark courtyard, and ran as hard as he could for the forest road.

He listened for the shouts of pursuers but could hear none yet. He wondered if perhaps he had hit Davud too hard.

Ryly spent an uneasy night in the forest not too far from the edge of the Baille territory; when morning came, he struck out at a rapid pace for the Baille-Clingert border. Joanne would be at the waterfall by Dorisrise—he hoped. For an instant he considered what would become of him if she had been playing him false, but he reached no answer. Could he return to the Bailles and marry Hella after all? He didn't think so.

The day grew warmer as he half trotted through the forest, following the series of trail-marks he had left to guide himself. When he reached the trysting place, it was not yet Dorisrise; Thomas alone was in the sky. Ryly sat by the water's edge and splashed himself to clean away the sweat of travel.

He heard footsteps. He looked up, hoping it might be Joanne. But it was Davud who appeared.

"So you followed me?"

Davud nodded. "I had to, Ryly."

"And I suppose you brought the whole tribe behind you, all of them foaming at the mouth and ready to stone me." Ryly sighed. "I guess I didn't hit you hard enough, then. You woke up too soon."

Davud's nose was swollen and slightly askew. He said, "I came alone. I want to try to talk you out of this crazy thing, Ryly. Nobody else knows about it yet."

"Good. Now you go back and forget anything I said to you last night."

"I can't do that," Davud said. "I can't let you mate with a—a *Clingert*. I came to bring you back to Baille land with me."

Ryly clenched his fists. He had no desire to fight with his phenotype-brother a second time, but if Davud was going to insist—

"Get away from me, Davud. Go back alone."

It was almost Dorisrise time, now. Ryly hoped he would be able to get Davud out of the way before Joanne reached their rendezvous. But Davud was shaking his head stubbornly. "Baille and Clingert shall not breed. Thomas set that law down for us in the beginning, and it can never be broken. It is—"

He stopped, jaw sagging, and pointed. Slowly Ryly turned. The first rays of Doris glinted blue in the flowing waterfall, and Joanne stood behind him.

"Which of you is Ryly?" she asked plaintively.

Ryly unfroze first. "I am," he said. "This is my phenotype-brother Davud. He came with me to—meet you. Davud, this is Joanne."

"Is *this* a Clingert?" Davud asked slowly. "But—but— Clanfather always said they were *ugly!* And —"

Ryly began to smile. Good old Davud was a true phenotype-brother after all; his reaction to Joanne on first sight was identical to Ryly's. It was heartwarming to see him react that way.

Joanne laughed, her special Clingert sort of laugh that Ryly had already grown to love. "He seems stunned. Just as stunned as you were, three days ago. Do all of you Bailles think we're ogres?"

Davud sat down heavily on a rotting stump. His face was very pale by the light of the double suns; he was shaking his head reflectively and seemed to be talking quietly to himself. At length he said, "All right. I apologize, Ryly. Now I see what you were talking about. *Now* I see!"

There was an overenthusiastic note in Davud's tone of voice that irked Ryly, but he refrained from voicing any annoyance. "What about Thomas and his laws now, Davud?" he said. "Now that you've seen a Clingert?"

"I take everything back," Davud murmured. "Everything."

Ryly glanced from his phenotype-brother to Joanne. "I guess we have his blessing, then. If—if you're willing to become an outcast from the Clingerts, that is."

Now it was Joanne's turn to look startled. "Outcast? For fulfilling the aim of the first Clingert?"

"What's that?"

"You mean you don't know?"

Ryly shook his head. "I don't have the faintest idea of what you're talking about."

"When it all started," she said patiently. "When the spaceship exploded and the Clingerts and Bailles were thrown free and landed on The World, hundreds of years ago, Jarl Clingert wanted to interbreed, but Thomas Baille wouldn't have any of it. He wanted to keep his line pure. So there hasn't been very much contact between Clingert and Baille since then, ever since the time the first Baille threatened without provocation to kill Jarl Clingert if he came within ten miles of—"

"Hold it," Ryly said. "It was Clingert who tried to kill Thomas Baille and marry Doris, but Thomas drove him off and—"

"No," said Joanne. "You've got it all backward. It was *Baille's* fault that—"

"Let's discuss ancient history some other time," Davud interjected suddenly. There was a curiously pained expression on his face. "Ryly, do you mind if I talk to you alone a moment?"

"Why—all right," Ryly said, surprised.

They drew a few feet farther away, and Ryly said, "Well? What do you think of her?"

"That's what I want to talk to you about," Davud whispered harshly. "I think she's far and away above the Baille women. She's so—*different*. Gentle but not weak, small but not flimsy—"

"I knew you'd like her, Davud."

"Not *like*," Davud groaned. "*Love*. I love her too, Ryly."

It came like a blow across the face. Ryly's eyes widened and stared into the equally blue ones of his phenotype-brother. The Baille genes had been duplicated perfectly among them, it seemed. In every respect.

"You can't mean that," Ryly said.

"I do. Dammit, I do. How can I help it?"

"We can't *both* have her, Davud. And I think I have priority. I—"

Davud gasped and seized him suddenly, spinning him around. Ryly looked, shut his eyes, touched his fingers lightly to his eyelids, and looked again. The mirage was still there. It was no illusion.

He saw two Joannes.

"Ryly? Davud? Meet Melena. Melena Clingert."

"Is she—your sister?" Ryly asked hoarsely. The two Clingerts were, at this distance, identical.

"My cousin," Joanne said. "I don't have any sisters." She grinned. "Melena was hiding near the far side of the waterfall. I brought her along to have a peek at Ryly. I've always been a show-off about some things."

Ryly and his phenotype-brother exchanged astonished glances.

"Of course," Ryly said softly. "We Bailles all look alike; why shouldn't the Clingerts? Three hundred years of inbreeding. Lord, they must all be identical!"

"More or less," Joanne said. "There are some minor variations but not many. Most of the unfixed genes in the clan were lost generations ago. As probably happened in your clan too. This was the thing that Jarl Clingert wanted to avoid, but when Thomas Baille refused to—"

"It was Clingert's treacherous ways that caused the whole thing," Ryly snapped. "Let's get that straight right now. Why, it's common knowledge!"

"Among whom? Among the Bailles, that's who— whom!" Joanne's eyes were blazing again, with the fury Ryly loved so much to see. "But why don't you listen to the Clingert side of the story for a change? You Bailles were always like that, shutting your ears to anything important. You—" She stopped in mid-breath. Very quietly she said, "I'm sorry, Ryly."

"It was my fault. I started the whole thing."

"No," she said, shaking her head. "I did, when I brought up the topic of—"

He smiled and touched a finger lightly to her lips. "Look," he said.

She looked. Davud and Melena had drawn to one side, standing on a moist, moss-covered patch of ground within the field of spray and foam of the waterfall. They were talking softly. It wasn't difficult to see by their faces what the topic of discussion was.

"We'll have to forget about ancient history now," Joanne said. "Forget all about what happened between Jarl Clingert and Thomas Baille four centuries ago."

Ryly took her hand. "We'll go somewhere else on The World," he said. "Start all over, build a new settlement. Just the four of us. And maybe we can recruit some others, if I can lure a few Bailles out here to meet Clingerts."

"And vice versa. The Clingert men hate the Bailles now too, you know. But that can stop. We'll breed the feuding out."

Ryly looked over at Davud and Melena, then back at Joanne. Everything looked incredibly lovely at that moment—the angular red leaves of the overhanging trees, the white spray of the falls, prismatically colored blue and gold by the sunlight, the quiet green clouds drifting above. He wanted to fix that moment in his mind forever.

He smiled. His mind was still full of insidious Clan-father-instilled legends of the early days on The World as seen through Baille eyes. But he could start forgetting them now.

Soon there would be a third clan on The World—a hybrid clan, both fair and dark, both short and tall.

And someday his descendants would be spinning legends about *him,* and how he had helped to found the clan, back in the misty time-shrouded days of the remote past.

Something Wild Is Loose

1.

The Vsiir got aboard the Earthbound ship by accident. It had absolutely no plans for taking a holiday on a wet, grimy planet like Earth. But it was in its metamorphic phase, undergoing the period of undisciplined change that began as winter came on, and it had shifted so far up-spectrum that Earthborn eyes couldn't see it. Oh, a really skilled observer might notice a slippery little purple flicker once in a while, a kind of snore, as the Vsiir momentarily dropped down out of the ultraviolet; but he'd have to know where to look, and when. The crewman who was responsible for putting the Vsiir on the ship never even considered the possibility that there might be something invisible sleeping atop one of the crates of cargo being hoisted into the ship's hold. He simply went down the row, slapping a floater-node on each crate and sending it gliding up the gravity well toward the open hatch. The fifth crate to go inside was the one on which the Vsiir had decided to take its nap. The spaceman didn't know that he had inadvertently given an alien organism a free ride to Earth. The Vsiir didn't know it, either, until the hatch was sealed and an oxygen-nitrogen atmosphere began to hiss from the vents. The Vsiir did not happen to breathe those gases, but, because it was in its time of metamorphosis, it was able to adapt itself quickly and nicely to the sour, prickly vapors seeping into its metabolic cells. The next

150

step was to fashion a set of full-spectrum scanners and learn something about its surroundings. Within a few minutes, the Vsiir was aware—

—that it was in a large, dark place that held a great many boxes containing various mineral and vegetable products of its world, mainly branches of the green-fire tree but also some other things of no comprehensible value to a Vsiir—

—that a double wall of curved metal enclosed this place—

—that just beyond this wall was a null-atmosphere zone, such as is found between one planet and another—

—that this therefore was a spaceship, heading rapidly away from the world of Vsiirs and in fact already some ten planetary diameters distant, with the gap growing alarmingly moment by moment—

—that it would be impossible, even for a Vsiir in metamorphosis, to escape from the spaceship at this point—

—and that, unless it could persuade the crew of the ship to halt and go back, it would be compelled to undertake a long and dreary voyage to a strange and probably loathsome world, where life would at best be highly inconvenient, and might present great dangers. It would find itself cut off painfully from the rhythm of its own civilization. It would miss the Festival of Changing. It would miss the Holy Eclipse. It would not be able to take part in next spring's Rising of the Sea. It would suffer in a thousand ways.

There were six human beings aboard the ship. Extending its perceptors, the Vsiir tried to reach their minds. Though humans had been coming to its planet for many years, it had never bothered making contact with them before; but it had never been in this much trouble before, either. It sent a foggy tendril of thought roving the corridors, looking for traces of human intelligence. Here?

A glow of electrical activity within a sphere of bone: a mind, a mind! A busy mind. But surrounded by a wall, apparently; the Vsiir rammed up against it and was thrust back. That was startling and disturbing. What kind of beings were these, whose minds were closed to ordinary contact? The Vsiir went on, hunting through the ship. Another mind: again closed. Another. Another. The Vsiir felt panic rising. Its mantle fluttered; its energy radiations dropped far down into the visual spectrum, then shot nervously toward much shorter waves. Even its physical form experienced a series of quick, involuntary metamorphoses, to the Vsiir's intense embarrassment. It did not get control of its body until it had passed from spherical to cubical to chaotic, and had become a gridwork of fibrous threads held together only by a pulsing strand of ego. Fiercely it forced itself back to the spherical form and resumed its search of the ship, dismally realizing that by now its native world was half a solar unit away. It was without hope now, but it continued to probe the minds of the crew, if only for the sake of thoroughness. Even if it made contact, though, how could it communicate the nature of its plight, and even if it communicated, why would the humans be disposed to help it? Yet it went on through the ship. And—

Here: an open mind. No wall at all. A miracle! The Vsiir rushed into close contact, overcome with joy and surprise, pouring out its predicament. *Please listen. Unfortunate non-human organism accidentally transported into this vessel during loading of cargo. Metabolically and psychologically unsuited for prolonged life on Earth. Begs pardon for inconvenience, wishes prompt return to home planet recently left, regrets disturbance in shipping schedule but hopes that this large favor will not prove impossible to grant. Do you comprehend my sending? Unfortunate non-human organism accidentally transported—*

2.

Lieutenant Falkirk had drawn the first sleep-shift after floatoff. It was only fair; Falkirk had knocked himself out processing the cargo during the loading stage, slapping the floater-nodes on every crate and feeding the transit manifests to the computer. Now that the ship was space-borne he could grab some rest while the other crewmen were handling the floatoff chores. So he settled down for six hours in the cradle as soon as they were on their way. Below him, the ship's six gravity-drinkers spun on their axes, gobbling inertia and pushing up the acceleration, and the ship floated Earthward at a velocity that would reach the galactic level before Falkirk woke. He drifted into drowsiness. A good trip: enough greenfire bark in the hold to see Earth through a dozen fits of the molecule plague, and plenty of other potential medicinals besides, along with a load of interesting mineral samples, and—Falkirk slept. For half an hour he enjoyed sweet slumber, his mind disengaged, his body loose.

Until a dark dream bubbled through his skull.

Deep purple sunlight, hot and somber. Something slippery tickling the edges of his brain. He lies on a broad white slab in a scorched desert. Unable to move. Getting harder to breathe. The gravity—a terrible pull, bending and breaking him, ripping his bones apart. Hooded figures moving around him, pointing, laughing, exchanging blurred comments in an unknown language. His skin melting and taking on a new texture: porcupine quills sprouting inside his flesh and forcing their way upward, poking out through every pore. Points of fire all over him. A thin scarlet hand, withered red fingers like crab-claws, hovering in front of his face. Scratching. Scratching. Scratching. His blood running among the quills, thick and sluggish. He shivers, struggling to sit up —lifts a hand, leaving pieces of quivering flesh stuck to the slab—sits up—

Wakes, trembling, screaming.

Falkirk's shout still sounded in his ears as his eyes adjusted to the light. Lieutenant Commander Rodriguez was holding his shoulders and shaking him.

"You all right?"

Falkirk tried to reply. Words wouldn't come. Hallucinatory shock, he realized, as part of his mind attempted to convince the other part that the dream was over. He was trained to handle crises: he ran through a quick disciplinary countdown and calmed himself, though he was still badly shaken. "Nightmare," he said hoarsely. "A beauty. Never had a dream with that kind of intensity before."

Rodriguez relaxed. Obviously he couldn't get very upset over a mere nightmare. "You want a pill?"

Falkirk shook his head. "I'll manage, thanks."

But the impact of the dream lingered. It was more than an hour before he got back to sleep, and then he fell into a light, restless doze, as if his mind were on guard against a return of those chilling fantasies. Fifty minutes before his programmed wake-up time, he was awakened by a ghastly shriek from the far side of the cabin.

Lieutenant Commander Rodriguez was having a nightmare.

3.

When the ship made floatdown on Earth a month later, it was, of course, put through the usual decontamination procedures before anyone or anything aboard it was allowed out of the starport. The outer hull got squirted with sealants designed to trap and smother any microorganism that might have hitchhiked from another world; the crewmen emerged through the safety pouch and went straight into a quarantine chamber without being exposed to the air; the ship's atmosphere was cycled into withdrawal chambers, where it underwent a thorough purification, and the entire interior of the vessel received a six-phase sterilization, beginning with fifteen minutes of hard vacuum and ending with an hour of neutron bombardment.

These procedures caused a certain degree of inconvenience for the Vsiir. It was already at the low end of its energy phase, due mainly to the repeated discouragements it had suffered in its attempts to communicate with the six humans. Now it was forced to adapt to a variety of unpleasant environments with no chance to rest between changes. Even the most adaptable of organisms can get tired. By the time the starport's decontamination team was ready to certify that the ship was wholly free of alien life-forms, the Vsiir was very, very tired indeed.

The oxygen-nitrogen atmosphere entered the hold once more. The Vsiir found it quite welcome, at least in contrast to all that had just been thrown at it. The hatch was open; stevedores were muscling the cargo crates into position to be floated across the field to the handling dome. The Vsiir took advantage of this moment to extrude some legs and scramble out of the ship. It found itself on a broad concrete apron rimmed by massive buildings. A yellow sun was shining in a blue sky; infrared was bouncing all over the place, but the Vsiir speedily made arrangements to deflect the excess. It also compensated immediately for the tinge of ugly hydrocarbons in the atmosphere, for the frightening noise level, and for the leaden feeling of homesickness that suddenly threatened its organic stability at the first sight of this unfamiliar, disheartening world. How to get home again? How to make contact, even? The Vsiir sensed nothing but closed minds—sealed like seeds in their shells. True, from time to time the minds of these humans opened, but even then they seemed unwilling to let the Vsiir's message get through.

Perhaps it would be different here. Perhaps those six were poor communicators, for some reason, and there would be more receptive minds available in this place. Perhaps. Perhaps. Close to despair, the Vsiir hurried across the field, and slipped into the first building in which it sensed open minds. There were hundreds of humans in it, occupying many levels, and the open minds were widely scattered. The Vsiir located the nearest one and, worriedly, earnestly, hopefully, touched the tip of its mind to the human's. *Please listen. I mean no harm. Am non-human organism arrived on your planet through unhappy circumstances, wishing only quick going back to own world—*

4.

The cardiac wing of Long Island Starport Hospital was on the ground floor, in the rear, where the patients could be given floater therapy without upsetting the gravitational ratios of the rest of the building. As always, the hospital was full—people were always coming in sick off starliners, and most of them were hospitalized right at the starport for their own safety—and the cardiac wing had more than its share. At the moment it held a dozen infarcts awaiting implant, nine post-implant recupes, five coronaries in emergency stasis, three ventricle-regrowth projects, an aortal patch job, and nine or ten assorted other cases. Most of the patients were floating, to keep down the gravitational strain on their damaged tissues—all but the regrowth people, who were under full Earthnorm gravity so that their new hearts would come in with the proper resilience and toughness. The hospital had a fine reputation and one of the lowest mortality rates in the hemisphere.

Losing two patients the same morning was a shock to the entire staff.

At 0917 the monitor flashed the red light for Mrs. Maldonado, eighty-seven, post-transplant and thus far doing fine. She had developed acute endocarditis coming back from a tour of the Jupiter system; at her age there wasn't enough vitality to sustain her through the slow business of growing a new heart with a genetic prod, but they'd given her a synthetic implant and for two weeks it had worked quite well. Suddenly, though, the hospital control center was getting a load of grim telemetry from Mrs. Maldonado's bed: valve action zero, blood pressure zero, respiration zero, pulse zero, everything zero, zero, zero. The EEG showed a violent lurch, as though she had received some abrupt and intense shock, followed by a minute or two of irregular action, followed by termination of brain activity. Long before any hospital personnel had reached her bedside, automatic revival equipment, both chemical and electrical, had gone to work on the patient, but she was beyond reach: a massive cerebral hemorrhage, coming totally without warning, had done irreversible damage.

At 0928 came the second outage: Mr. Guinness, fifty-one, three days past surgery for a coronary embolism. The same series of events. A severe jolt to the nervous system, an immediate and fatal physiological response. Resuscitation procedures negative. No one on the staff had any plausible explanation for Mr. Guinness' death. Like Mrs. Maldonado, he had been sleeping peacefully, all vital signs good, until the moment of the fatal seizure.

"As though someone had come up and yelled *boo* in their ears," one doctor muttered, puzzling over the charts. He pointed to the wild EEG track. "Or as if they'd had unbearably vivid nightmares and couldn't take the sensory overload. But no one was making noise in the ward. And nightmares aren't contagious."

5.

Dr. Peter Mookherji, resident in neuropathology, was beginning his morning rounds on the hospital's sixth level when the soft voice of his annunciator, taped behind his left ear, asked him to report to the Quarantine Building immediately. Dr. Mookherji scowled. "Can't it wait? This is my busiest time of day, and—"

"You are asked to come at once."

"Look, I've got a girl in a coma here, due for her teletherapy session in fifteen minutes, and she's counting on seeing me. I'm her only link to the world. If I'm not there when—"

"You are asked to come at once, Dr. Mookherji."

"Why do the quarantine people need a neuropathologist in such a hurry? Let me take care of the girl, at least, and in forty-five minutes they can have me."

"Dr. Mookherji—"

It didn't pay to argue with a machine. Mookherji forced his temper down. Short tempers ran in his family, along with a fondness for torrid curries and a talent for telepathy. Glowering, he grabbed a data terminal, identified himself, and told the hospital's control center to reprogram his entire morning schedule. "Build in a half-hour postponement somehow," he snapped. "I can't help it—

see for yourself. I've been requisitioned by the quarantine staff." The computer was thoughtful enough to have a rollerbuggy waiting for him when he emerged from the hospital. It whisked him across the starport to the Quarantine Building in three minutes, but he was still angry when he got there. The scanner at the door ticked off his badge and one of the control center's innumerable voice-outputs told him solemnly, "You are expected in Room 403, Dr. Mookherji."

Room 403 turned out to be a two-sector interrogation office. The rear sector of the room was part of the building's central quarantine core, and the front sector belonged to the public-access part of the building, with a thick glass wall in between. Six haggard-looking spacemen were slouched on sofas behind the wall, and three members of the starport's quarantine staff paced about in the front. Mookherji's irritation ebbed when he saw that one of the quarantine men was an old medical-school friend, Lee Nakadai. The slender Japanese was a year older than Mookherji—twenty-nine to twenty-eight; they met for lunch occasionally at the starport commissary, and they had double-dated a pair of Filipino twins earlier in the year, but the pressure of work had kept them apart for months. Nakadai got down to business quickly now. "Pete, have you ever heard of an epidemic of nightmares?"

Indicating the men behind the quarantine wall, Nakadai said, "These fellows came in an hour and a half ago from Norton's Star. Brought back a cargo of greenfire bark. Physically they check out to five decimal places, and I'd release them except for one funny thing. They're all in a bad state of nervous exhaustion, which they say is the result of having had practically no sleep during their whole month-long return trip. And the reason for that is that they were having nightmares—every one of them—real mind-wrecking killer dreams, whenever they tried to sleep. It sounded so peculiar that I thought we'd better run a neuropath checkup, in case they've picked up some kind of cerebral infection."

Mookherji frowned. "For this you get me out of my ward on emergency requisition, Lee?"

"Talk to them," Nakadai said. "Maybe it'll scare you a little."

Mookherji glanced at the spacemen. "All right," he said. "What about these nightmares?"

A tall, bony-looking officer who introduced himself as Lieutenant Falkirk said, "I was the first victim—right after floatoff. I almost flipped. It was like, well, something touching my mind, filling it with weird thoughts. And everything absolutely real while it was going on—I thought I was choking, I thought my body was changing into something alien, I felt my blood running out my pores—" Falkirk shrugged. "Like any sort of bad dream, I guess, only ten times as vivid. Fifty times. A few hours later Lieutenant Commander Rodriguez had the same kind of dream. Different images, same effect. And then, one by one, as the others took their sleep-shifts, they started to wake up screaming. Two of us ended up spending three weeks on happy-pills. We're pretty stable men, doctor—we're trained to take almost anything. But I think a civilian would have cracked up for good with dreams like those. Not so much the images as the intensity, the realness of it."

"And these dreams recurred throughout the voyage?" Mooherji asked.

"Every shift. It got so we were afraid to doze off, because we knew the devils would start crawling through our heads when we did. Or we'd put ourselves real down on sleeper-tabs. And even so we'd have the dreams, with our minds doped to a level where you wouldn't imagine dreams would happen. A plague of nightmares, doctor. An epidemic."

"When was the last episode?"

"The final sleep-shift before floatdown."

"You haven't gone to sleep, any of you, since leaving the ship?"

"No," Falkirk said.

One of the other spacemen said, "Maybe he didn't make it clear to you, Doctor. These were killer dreams. They were mind-crackers. We were lucky to get home sane. If we did."

Mookherji drummed his fingertips together, rummaging through his experience for some parallel case. He couldn't find any. He knew of mass hallucinations, plenty of them, episodes in which whole mobs had persuaded themselves they had seen gods, demons, miracles, the dead walking, fiery symbols in the sky. But a series of hallucinations coming in sequence, shift after shift, to an entire crew of tough, pragmatic spacemen? It didn't make sense.

Nakadai said, "Pete, the men had a guess about what might have done it to them. Just a wild idea, but maybe—"

"What is it?"

Falkirk laughed uneasily. "Actually, it's pretty fantastic, Doctor."

"Go ahead."

"Well, that something from the planet came aboard the ship with us. Something, well, telepathic. Which fiddled around with our minds whenever we went to sleep. What we felt as nightmares was maybe this thing inside our heads."

"Possibly it rode all the way back to Earth with us," another spaceman said. "It could still be aboard the ship. Or loose in the city by now."

"The Invisible Nightmare Menace?" Mookherji said,

with a faint smile. "I doubt that I can buy that."

"There *are* telepathic creatures," Falkirk pointed out.

"I know," Mookherji said sharply. "I happen to be one myself."

"I'm sorry, Doctor, if—"

"But that doesn't lead me to look for telepaths under every bush. I'm not ruling out your alien menace, mind you. But I think it's a lot more likely that you picked up some kind of inflammation of the brain out there. A virus disease, a type of encephalitis that shows itself in the form of chronic hallucinations." The spacemen looked troubled. Obviously they would rather be victims of an unknown monster preying on them from outside than of an unknown virus lodged in their brains. Mookherji went on, "I'm not saying that's what it is, either. I'm just tossing around hypotheses. We'll know more after we've run some tests." Checking his watch, he said to Nakadai, "Lee, there's not much more I can find out right now, and I've got to get back to my patients. I want these fellows plugged in for the full series of neuropsychological checkouts. Have the outputs relayed to my office as they come in. Run the tests in staggered series and start letting the men go to sleep, two at a time, after each series—I'll send over a technician to help you rig the telemetry. I want to be notified immediately if there's any nightmare experience."

"Right."

"And get them to sign telepathy releases. I'll give them a preliminary mind-probe this evening after I've had a chance to study the clinical findings. Maintain absolute quarantine, of course. This thing might just be infectious. Play it very safe."

Nakadai nodded. Mookherji flashed a professional smile at the six somber spacemen and went out, brooding. A nightmare virus? Or a mind-meddling alien organism that no one can see? He wasn't sure which notion he liked less. Probably, though, there was some prosaic and un-startling explanation for that month of bad dreams—contaminated food supplies, or something funny in the atmosphere recycler. A simple, mundane explanation.

Probably.

6.

The first time it happened, the Vsiir was not sure what had actually taken place. It had touched a human mind; there had been an immediate vehement reaction; the Vsiir had pulled back, alarmed by the surging fury of the response, and then, a moment later, had been unable to locate the mind at all. Possibly it was some defense mechanism, the Vsiir thought, by which the humans guarded their minds against intruders. But that made little sense, since the humans' minds were quite effectively guarded most of the time anyway. Aboard the ship, whenever the Vsiir had managed to slip past the walls that shielded the minds of the crewmen, it had always encountered a great deal of turbulence—plainly these humans did not enjoy mental contact with a Vsiir—but never this complete shutdown, this total cutoff of signal. Puzzled, the Vsiir tried again, reaching toward an open mind situated not far from where the one that had vanished had been. *Kindly attention, a moment of consideration for confused otherworldly individual, victim of unhappy circumstances, who—*

Again the violent response: a sudden tremendous flare of mental energy, a churning blaze of fear and pain and shock. And again, moments later, complete silence, as though the human had retreated behind an impermeable barrier. *Where are you? Where did you go?* The Vsiir, troubled, took the risk of creating an optical receptor that worked in the visual spectrum—and that therefore would itself be visible to humans—and surveyed the scene. It saw a human on a bed, completely surrounded by intricate machinery. Colored lights were flashing. Other humans, looking agitated, were rushing toward the bed. The human on the bed lay quite still, not even moving when a metal arm descended and jabbed a long bright needle into his chest.

Suddenly the Vsiir understood.

The two humans must have experienced termination of existence!

Hastily the Vsiir dissolved its visual-spectrum receptor and retreated to a sheltered corner to consider what had happened. *Datum:* two humans had died. *Datum:* each had undergone termination immediately after receiving a mental transmission from the Vsiir. *Problem:* had the mental transmission brought about the terminations?

The possibility that the Vsiir might have destroyed two lives was shocking and appalling, and such a chill went through its body that it shrank into a tight, hard ball, with all thought-processes snarled. It needed several minutes to return to a fully functional state. If its attempts at communicating with these humans produced such terrible effects, the Vsiir realized, then its prospects of finding help on this planet were slim. How could it dare risk trying to contact other humans, if—

A comforting thought surfaced. The Vsiir realized that it was jumping to a hasty conclusion on the basis of sketchy evidence, while overlooking some powerful arguments against that conclusion. All during the voyage to this world the Vsiir had been making contact with humans, the six crewmen, and none of *them* had terminated. That was ample evidence that humans could withstand contact with a Vsiir mind. Therefore contact alone could not have caused these two deaths.

Possibly it was only coincidental that the Vsiir had

approached two humans in succession that were on the
verge of termination. Was this the place where humans
were brought when their time of termination was near?
Would the terminations have happened even if the Vsiir
had not tried to make contact? Was the attempt at contact just enough of a drain on dwindling energies to push
the two over the edge into termination? The Vsiir did
not know. It was uncomfortably conscious of how many
important facts it lacked. Only one thing was certain: its
time was running short. If it did not find help soon,
metabolic decay was going to set in, followed by metamorphic rigidity, followed by a fatal loss in adaptability, followed by . . . termination.

The Vsiir had no choice. Continuing its quest for contact with a human was its only hope of survival. Cautiously, timidly, the Vsiir again began to send out its
probes, looking for a properly receptive mind. This one
was walled. So was this. And all these: no entrance, no
entrance! The Vsiir wondered if the barriers these humans possessed were designed merely to keep out in-
truding non-human consciousnesses, or actually shielded
each human against mental contact of all kinds, including contact with other humans. If any human-to-human
contact existed, the Vsiir had not detected it, either in
this building or aboard the spaceship. What a strange
race!

Perhaps it would be best to try a different level of this
building. The Vsiir flowed easily under a closed door and
up a service staircase to a higher floor. Once more it
sent forth its probes. A closed mind here. And here. And
here. And then a receptive one. The Vsiir prepared to
send its message. For safety's sake it stepped down the
power of its transmission, letting a mere wisp of thought
curl forth. *Do you hear? Stranded extraterrestrial being
is calling. Seeks aid. Wishes—*

From the human came a sharp, stinging displeasure-response, wordless but unmistakably hostile. The Vsiir at once withdrew. It waited, terrified, fearing that it had caused another termination. No: the human mind continued to function, although it was no longer open, but surrounded by the sort of barrier humans normally wore. Drooping, dejected, the Vsiir crept away. Failure, again. Not even a moment of meaningful mind-to-mind contact. Was there no way to reach these people? Dismally, the Vsiir resumed its search for a receptive mind. What else could it do?

7.

The visit to the quarantine building had taken forty minutes out of Dr. Mookherji's morning schedule. That bothered him. He couldn't blame the quarantine people for getting upset over the six spacemen's tale of chronic hallucinations, but he didn't think the situation, mysterious as it was, was grave enough to warrant calling him in on an emergency basis. Whatever was troubling the spacemen would eventually come to light; meanwhile they were safely isolated from the rest of the starport. Nakadai should have run more tests before bothering him. And he resented having to steal time from his patients.

But as he began his belated morning rounds, Mookherji calmed himself with a deliberate effort: it wouldn't do him or his patients any good if he visited them while still loaded with tensions and irritations. He was supposed to be a healer, not a spreader of anxieties. He spent a moment going through a de-escalation routine, and by the time he entered the first patient's room—that of Satina Ransom—he was convincingly relaxed and amiable.

Satina lay on her left side, eyes closed, a slender girl of sixteen with a fragile-looking face and long, soft, straw-colored hair. A spidery network of monitoring systems surrounded her. She had been unconscious for sixteen months, twelve of them here in the starport's neuropathology ward and the last six under Mookherji's care. As a holiday treat, her parents had taken her to one of the resorts on Titan during the best season for viewing Saturn's rings; with great difficulty they had succeeded in booking reservations at Galileo Dome, and were there on the grim day when a violent Titanquake ruptured the dome and exposed a thousand tourists to the icy moon's poisonous methane atmosphere. Satina was one of the lucky ones: she got no more than a couple of whiffs of the stuff before a dome guide with whom she'd been talking managed to get a breathing mask over her face. She survived. Her mother, father, and younger brother didn't. But she had never regained consciousness after collapsing at the moment of the disaster. Months of examination on Earth had shown that her brief methane inhalation hadn't caused any major brain damage; organically there seemed to be nothing wrong with her, but she refused to wake up. A shock reaction, Mookherji believed: she would rather go on dreaming forever than return to the living nightmare that consciousness had become. He had been able to reach her mind telepathically, but so far he had been unable to cleanse her of the trauma of that catastrophe and bring her back to the waking world.

Now he prepared to make contact. There was nothing easy or automatic about his telepathy; "reading" minds was strenuous work for him, as difficult and as taxing as running a cross-country race or memorizing a lengthy part in *Hamlet*. Despite the fears of laymen, he had no way of scanning anyone's intimate thoughts with a cas-

ual glance. To enter another mind, he had to go through
an elaborate procedure of warming up and reaching out,
and even so it was a slow business to tune in on somebody's "wavelength," with little coherent information
coming across until the ninth or tenth attempt. The gift
had been in the Mookherji family for at least a dozen
generations, helped along by shrewdly planned mar-
riages designed to conserve the precious gene; he was
more adept than any of his ancestors, yet it might take
another century or two of Mookherjis to produce a really
potent telepath. At least he was able to make good use
of such talent for mind-contact as he had. He knew that
many members of his family in earlier times had been
forced to hide their gift from those about them, back
in India, lest they be classed with vampires and were-
wolves and cast out of society.

Gently he placed his dark hand on Satina's pale wrist.
Physical contact was necessary to attain the mental link-
age. He concentrated on reaching her. After months of
teletherapy, her mind was sensitized to his; he was able
to skip the intermediate steps and, once he was warmed
up, could plunge straight into her troubled soul. His eyes
were closed. He saw a swirl of pearl-gray fog before him:
Satina's mind. He thrust himself into it, entering easily.
Up from the depths of her spirit swam a question mark.

—*Who is it? Doctor?*

—*Me, yes. How are you today, Satina?*

—*Fine. Just fine.*

—*Been sleeping well?*

—*It's so peaceful here, Doctor.*

—*Yes. Yes, I imagine it is. But you ought to see how
it is here. A wonderful summer day. The sun in the blue
sky. Everything in bloom. A perfect day for swimming,
eh? Wouldn't you like a swim?* He puts all the force of
his concentration into images of swimming: a cold moun-

tain stream, a deep pool at the base of a creamy waterfall, the sudden delightful shock of diving in, the crystal
flow tingling against her warm skin, the laughter of her
friends, the splashing, the swift powerful strokes carrying her to the far shore—

—*I'd rather stay where I am,* she tells him.

—*Maybe you'd like to go floating instead?* He summons
the sensations of free flight: a floater-node fastened to
her belt, lifting her serenely to an altitude of a hundred
feet, and off she goes, drifting over fields and valleys,
her friends beside her, her body totally relaxed, weight-
less, soaring on the updrafts, rising until the ground is
a checkerboard of brown and green, looking down on the
tiny houses and the comical cars, now crossing a shim-
mering silvery lake, now hovering over a dark, somber
forest of thick-packed spruce, now simply lying on her
back, legs crossed, hands clasped behind her head, the
sunlight bright on her cheeks, three hundred feet of
nothingness underneath her—

But Satina doesn't take his bait. She prefers to stay
where she is. The temptations of floating are not strong
enough.

Mookherji does not have enough energy left to try a
third attempt at luring her out of her coma. Instead he
shifts to a purely medical function and tries to probe for
the source of the trauma that has cut her off from the
world. The fright, no doubt; and the terrible crack in the
dome, spelling the end to all security; and the sight of
her parents and brother dying before her eyes; and the
swampy reek of Titan's atmosphere hitting her nostrils
—all of those things, no doubt. But people have re-
bounded from worse calamities. Why does she insist on
withdrawing from life? Why not come to terms with
the dreadful past, and accept existence again?

But she fights him. Her defenses are fierce; she does

not want him meddling with her mind. All of their sessions have ended this way: Satina clinging to her retreat, Satina blocking any shot at knocking her free of her self-imposed prison. He has gone on hoping that one day she will lower her guard. But this is not to be the day. Wearily, he pulls back from the core of her mind and talks to her on a shallower level.

—*You ought to be getting back to school, Satina.*

—*Not yet. It's been such a short vacation!*

—*Do you know how long?*

—*About three weeks, isn't it?*

—*Sixteen months so far,* he tells her.

—*That's impossible. We just went away to Titan a little while ago—the week before Christmas, wasn't it, and—*

—*Satina, how old are you?*

—*I'll be fifteen in April.*

—*Wrong,* he tells her. *That April's been here and gone, and so has the next one. You were sixteen two months ago. Sixteen, Satina.*

—*That can't be true, Doctor. A girl's sixteenth birthday is something special, don't you know that? My parents are going to give me a big party. All my friends invited. And a nine-piece robot orchestra with synthesizers. And I know that that hasn't happened yet, so how can I be sixteen?*

His reservoir of strength is almost drained. His mental signal is weak. He cannot find the energy to tell her that she is blocking reality again, that her parents are dead, that time is passing while she lies here, that it is too late for a Sweet Sixteen party.

—*We'll talk about it . . . another time, Satina. I'll . . . see . . . you . . . again . . . tomorrow. . . . Tomorrow . . . morning. . . .*

—*Don't go so soon, Doctor!* But he can no longer hold the contact, and lets it break.

Releasing her, Mookherji stood up, shaking his head. A shame, he thought. A damned shame. He went out of the room on trembling legs, and paused a moment in the hall, propping himself against a closed door and mopping his sweaty forehead. He was getting nowhere with Satina. After the initial encouraging period of contact, he had failed entirely to lessen the intensity of her coma. She had settled quite comfortably into her delusive world of withdrawal, and, telepathy or no, he could find no way to blast her loose.

He took a deep breath. Fighting back a growing mood of bleak discouragement, he went toward the next patient's room.

8.

The operation was going smoothly. Two dozen third-year medical students occupied the observation deck of the surgical gallery on the starport hospital's third floor, studying Dr. Hammond's expert technique by direct viewing and by simultaneous microamplified relay to their individual desk-screens. The patient, a brain-tumor victim in his late sixties, was visible only as a head and shoulders protruding from a life-support chamber. His scalp had been shaved; blue lines and dark-red dots were painted on it to indicate the inner contours of the skull, as previously determined by short-range sonar-bounces; the surgeon had finished the job of positioning the lasers that would excise the tumor. The hard part was over. Nothing remained except to bring the lasers to full power and send their fierce, precise bolts of light slicing into the patient's brain. Cranial surgery of this kind was entirely bloodless; there was no need to cut through skin and bone to expose the tumor, for the beams of the lasers, calibrated to a millionth of an inch, would penetrate through minute openings and, playing on the tumor from different sides, would destroy the malignant growth without harming a bit of the surrounding healthy brain tissue. Planning was everything in an operation like this. Once the exact outlines of the tumor were determined, and the surgical lasers were mounted at the correct angles, any intern could finish the job.

For Dr. Hammond it was a routine procedure. He had performed a hundred operations of this kind in the past year alone. He gave the signal; the warning light glowed on the laser rack; the students in the gallery leaned forth expectantly—

And, just as the lasers' glittering fire leaped toward the operating table, the face of the anesthetized patient contorted weirdly, as though some terrifying dream had come drifting up out of the depths of the man's drugged mind. His nostrils flared; his lips drew back; his eyes opened wide; he seemed to be trying to scream; he moved convulsively, twisting his head to one side. The lasers bit deep into the patient's left temple, far from the indicated zone of the tumor. The right side of his face began to sag, all muscles paralyzed. The medical students looked at each other in bewilderment. Dr. Hammond, stunned, retained enough presence of mind to kill the lasers with a quick swipe of his hand. Then, gripping the operating table with both hands in his agitation, he peered at the dials and meters that told him the details of the botched operation. The tumor remained intact; a vast sector of the patient's brain had been devastated. "Impossible," Hammond muttered. What could goad a patient under anesthesia into jumping around like that? "Impossible. Impossible." He strode to the end of the table and checked the readings on the life-support chamber. The question now was not

whether the brain tumor would be successfully removed; the immediate question was whether the patient
was going to survive.

9.

By four that afternoon Mookherji had finished most
of his chores. He had seen every patient; he had brought
his progress charts up to date; he had fed a prognosis
digest to the master computer that was the starport
hospital's control center; he had even found time for a
gulped lunch. Ordinarily, now, he could take the next
four hours off, going back to his spartan room in the
residents' building at the edge of the starport complex
for a nap, or dropping in at the recreation center to
have a couple of rounds of floater-tennis, or looking in
at the latest cube-show, or whatever. His next round of
patient-visiting didn't begin until eight in the evening.
But he couldn't relax: there was that business of the
quarantined spacemen to worry about. Nakadai had been
sending test outputs over since two o'clock, and now
they were stacked deep in Mookherji's data terminal.
Nothing had carried an *urgent* flag, so Mookherji had
simply let the reports pile up; but now he felt he ought
to have a look. He tapped the keys of the terminal, re-
questing printouts, and Nakadai's outputs began to slide
from the slot.

Mookherji ruffled through the yellow sheets. Reflexes,
synapse charge, degree of neural ionization, endocrine
balances, visual response, respiratory & circulatory,
cerebral molecular exchange, sensory percepts, EEG
both enhanced and minimated. . . . No, nothing unusual here. It was plain from the tests that the six men
who had been to Norton's Star were badly in need of a
vacation—frayed nerves, blurred reflexes—but there

was no indication of anything more serious than chronic loss of sleep. He couldn't detect signs of brain lesions, infection, nerve damage, or other organic disabilities.

Why the nightmares, then?

He tapped out the phone number of Nakadai's office. "Quarantine," a crisp voice said almost at once, and moments later Nakadai's lean, tawny face appeared on the screen. "Hello, Pete. I was just going to call you."

Mookherji said, "I didn't finish up until a little while ago. But I've been through the outputs you sent over. Lee, there's nothing here."

"As I thought."

"What about the men? You were supposed to call me if any of them went into nightmares."

"None of them have," Nakadai said. "Falkirk and Rodriguez have been sleeping since eleven. Like lambs. Schmidt and Carroll were allowed to conk out at half past one. Webster and Schiavone hit the cots at three. All six are still snoring away, sleeping like they haven't slept in years. I've got them loaded with equipment and everything's reading perfectly normal. You want me to shunt the data to you?"

"Why bother? If they aren't hallucinating, what'll I learn?"

"Does that mean you plan to skip the mind-probes tonight?"

"I don't know," Mookherji said, shrugging. "I suspect there's no point in it, but let's leave that part open. I'll be finishing my evening rounds about eleven, and if there's some reason to get into the heads of those spacemen then, I will." He frowned. "But look—didn't they say that each one of them went into the nightmares on *every single sleep-shift?*"

"Right."

"And here they are, sleeping outside the ship for the

first time since the nightmares started, and none of them having any trouble at all. And no sign of possible hallucinogenic brain lesions. You know something, Lee? I'm starting to come around to a very silly hypothesis that those men proposed this morning."

"That the hallucinations were caused by some unseen alien being?" Nakadai asked.

"Something like that. Lee, what's the status of the ship they came in on?"

"It's been through all the routine purification checks, and now it's sitting in an isolation vector until we have some idea of what's going on."

"Would I be able to get aboard it?" Mookherji asked.

"I suppose so, yes, but—why—?"

"On the wild shot that something external caused those nightmares, and that that something may still be aboard the ship. And perhaps a low-level telepath like myself will be able to detect its presence. Can you set up clearance fast?"

"Within ten minutes," Nakadai said. "I'll pick you up."

Nakadai came by shortly in a rollerbuggy. As they headed out toward the landing field, he handed Mookherji a crumpled spacesuit and told him to put it on.

"What for?"

"You may want to breathe inside the ship. Right now it's full of vacuum—we decided it wasn't safe to leave it under atmosphere. Also it's still loaded with radiation from the decontamination process. Okay?"

Mookherji struggled into the suit.

They reached the ship: a standard interstellar null-gravity-drive job, looking small and lonely in its corner of the field. A robot cordon kept it under isolation, but, tipped off by the control center, the robots let the two doctors pass. Nakadai remained outside; Mookherji crawled into the safety pouch and, after the hatch had gone through its admission cycle, entered the ship. He moved cautiously from cabin to cabin, like a man walking in a forest that was said to have a jaguar in every tree. While looking about, he brought himself as quickly as possible up to full telepathic receptivity, and, wide open, awaited telepathic contact with anything that might be lurking in the ship.

—*Go on. Do your worst.*

Complete silence on all mental wavelengths. Mookherji prowled everywhere: the cargo hold, the crew cabins, the drive compartment. Everything empty, everything still. Surely he would have been able to detect the presence of a telepathic creature in here, no matter how alien; if it was capable of reaching the mind of a sleeping spaceman, it could reach the mind of a waking telepath as well. After fifteen minutes he left the ship, satisfied.

"Nothing there," he told Nakadai. "We're still nowhere."

10.

The Vsiir was growing desperate. It had been roaming this building all day; judging by the quality of the solar radiation coming through the windows, night was beginning to fall now. And, though there were open minds on every level of the structure, the Vsiir had had no luck in making contact. At least there had been no more terminations. But it was the same story here as on the ship: whenever the Vsiir touched a human mind, the reaction was so negative as to make communication impossible. And yet the Vsiir went on and on and on, to mind after mind, unable to believe that this whole planet did not hold a single human to whom it could tell its story. It hoped it was not doing severe damage to these minds it was approaching; but it had its own fate to consider.

Perhaps this mind would be the one. The Vsiir started once more to tell its tale—

11.

Half past nine at night. Dr. Peter Mookherji, bloodshot, tense, hauled himself through his neuropathological responsibilities. The ward was full: a schizoid collapse, a catatonic freeze, Satina in her coma, half a dozen routine hysterias, a couple of paralysis cases, an aphasic, and plenty more, enough to keep him going for sixteen hours a day and strain his telepathic powers, not to mention his conventional medical skills, to their limits. Someday the ordeal of residency would be over; someday he'd be quit of this hospital, and would set up private practice on some sweet tropical isle, and commute to Bombay on weekends to see his family, and spend his holidays on planets of distant stars, like any prosperous medical specialist. . . . Someday. He tried to banish such lavish fantasies from his mind. If you're going to look forward to anything, he told himself, look forward to midnight. To sleep. Beautiful, beautiful sleep. And then in the morning it all begins again, Satina and the coma, the schizoid, the catatonic, the aphasic . . .

As he stepped into the hall, going from patient to patient, his annunciator said, "Dr. Mookherji, please report at once to Dr. Bailey's office."

Bailey? The head of the neuropathology department, still hitting the desk this late? What now? But of course there was no ignoring such a summons. Mookherji notified the control center that he had been called off his rounds, and made his way quickly down the corridor to the frosted-glass door marked SAMUEL F. BAILEY, M.D.

He found at least half the neuropath staff there already: four of the other senior residents, most of the interns, even a few of the high-level doctors. Bailey, a puffy-faced, sandy-haired, fiftyish man of formidable professional standing, was thumbing a sheaf of outputs and scowling. He gave Mookherji a faint nod by way of greeting. They were not on the best of terms; Bailey, somewhat old-school in his attitudes, had not made a good adjustment to the advent of telepathy as a tool in the treatment of mental disturbance. "As I was just saying," Bailey began, "these reports have been accumulating all day, and they've all been dumped on me, God knows why. Listen: two cardiac patients under sedation undergo sudden violent shocks, described by one doctor as sensory overloads. One reacts with cardiac arrest, the other with cerebral hemorrhage. Both die. A patient being treated for endocrine restabilization develops a runaway adrenalin flow while asleep, and gets a six-month setback. A patient undergoing brain surgery starts jumping around on the operating table, despite adequate anesthesia, and gets badly carved up by the lasers. Et cetera. Serious problems like this all over the hospital today. Computer check of general EEG patterns shows that fourteen patients, other than those mentioned, have experienced exceptionally severe episodes of nightmare in the last eleven hours, nearly all of them of such impact that the patient has sustained some degree of psychic damage and often actual physiological harm. Control center reports no case histories of previous epidemics of bad dreams. No reason to suspect a widespread dietary imbalance or similar cause for the outbreak. Nevertheless, sleeping patients are continuing to suffer, and those whose condition is particularly critical may be exposed to grave risks. Effective immediately, sedation of critical patients has been interrupted where feasible, and sleep schedules of other patients have been rearranged, but this is obviously not an expedient that is going to do much good if this outbreak continues into tomorrow." Bailey paused, glanced around the room, let his gaze rest on Mookherji. "Control center has offered one hypothesis: that a psychopathic individual with strong telepathic powers is at large in the hospital, preying on sleeping patients and transmitting images to them that take the form of horrifying nightmares. Mookherji, what do you make of that idea?"

Mookherji said, "It's perfectly feasible, I suppose, although I can't imagine why any telepath would want to go around distributing nightmares. But has control center correlated any of this with the business over at the quarantine building?"

Bailey stared at his output slips. "What business is that?"

"Six spacemen who came in early this morning, reporting that they'd all suffered chronic nightmares on their voyage homeward. Dr. Lee Nakadai's been testing them; he called me in as a consultant, but I couldn't discover anything useful. I imagine there are some late reports from Nakadai in my office, but—"

Bailey said, "Control center seems only to be concerned about events in the hospital, not in the starport complex as a whole. And if your six spacemen had their nightmares during their voyage, there's no chance that their symptoms are going to find their way onto—"

"That's just it!" Mookherji cut in. "They had their nightmares in space. But they've been asleep since morning, and Nakadai says they're resting peacefully. Meanwhile an outbreak of hallucinations has started over here. Which means that whatever was bothering them during their voyage has somehow got loose in the hospital today—some sort of entity capable of stirring up such dreams that they bring veteran spacemen to the edge of nervous breakdowns and can seriously injure or even kill someone in poor health." He realized that Bailey was looking at him strangely, and that Bailey was not the only one. In a more restrained tone, Mookherji said, "I'm sorry if this sounds fantastic to you. I've been checking it out all day, so I've had some time to get used to the concept. And things began to fit together for me just now. I'm not saying that my idea is necessarily correct. I'm simply saying that it's a reasonable notion, that it links up with the spacemen's own idea of what was bothering them, that it corresponds to the shape of the situation— and that it deserves a decent investigation if we're going to stop this stuff before we lose some more patients."

"All right, Doctor," Bailey said. "How do you propose to conduct the investigation?"

Mookherji was shaken by that. He had been on the go all day; he was ready to fold. Here was Bailey abruptly putting him in charge of this snark-hunt, without even asking! But he saw there was no way to refuse. He was the only telepath on the staff. And, if the supposed creature really was at large in the hospital, how could it be tracked except by a telepath?

Fighting back his fatigue, Mookherji said rigidly, "Well, I'd want a chart of all the nightmare cases, to begin with, a chart showing the location of each victim and the approximate time of onset of hallucination—"

12.

They would be preparing for the Festival of Changing now, the grand climax of the winter. Thousands of Vsiirs in the metamorphic phase would be on their way toward the Valley of Sand, toward that great natural amphitheater where the holiest rituals were performed. By now the firstcomers would already have taken up their positions, facing the west, waiting for the sunrise. Gradually the rows would fill as Vsiirs came in from every part of the planet, until the golden valley was thick with them, Vsiirs that constantly shifted their energy-levels, dimensional extensions, and inner resonances, shuttling gloriously through the final joyous moments of the season of metamorphosis, competing with one another in a gentle way to display the greatest variety of form, the most dynamic cycle of physical changes—and, as the first red rays of the sun crept past the Needle, the celebrants would grow even more frenzied, dancing and leaping and transforming themselves with total abandon, purging themselves of the winter's flamboyance as the season of stability swept across the world. And finally, in the full blaze of sunlight, they would turn to one another in renewed kinship, embracing, and—

The Vsiir tried not to think about it. But it was hard to repress that sense of loss, that pang of nostalgia. The pain grew more intense with every moment. No imaginable miracle would get the Vsiir home in time for the Festival of Changing, it knew, and yet it could not really believe that such a calamity had befallen it.

Trying to touch minds with humans was useless. Perhaps if it assumed a form visible to them, and let itself be noticed, and *then* tried to open verbal communication—

But the Vsiir was so small, and these humans were so large. The dangers were great. The Vsiir, clinging to a wall and carefully keeping its wavelength well beyond the ultraviolet, weighed one risk against another, and, for the moment, did nothing.

13.

"All right," Mookherji said foggily, a little before midnight. "I think we've got the trail clear now." He sat before a wall-sized screen on which the control center had thrown a three-dimensional schematic plan of the hospital. Bright red dots marked the place of each nightmare incident, yellow dashes the probable path of the unseen alien creature. "It came in the side way, probably, straight off the ship, and went into the cardiac wing first. Mrs. Maldonado's bed here, Mr. Guinness' over here, eh? Then it went up to the second level, coming around to the front wing and impinging on the minds of patients here and here and here between ten and eleven in the morning. There were no reported episodes of hallucination in the next hour and ten minutes, but then came that nasty business in the third-level surgical gallery, and after that—" Mookherji's aching eyes closed a moment; it seemed to him that he could still see the red dots and yellow dashes. He forced himself to go on, tracing the rest of the intruder's route for his audience of doctors and hospital security personnel. At last he said, "That's it. I figure that the thing must be somewhere between the fifth and eighth levels by now. It's moving much more slowly than it did this morning, possibly running out of energy. What we have to do is keep the hospital's wing tightly sealed to prevent its free movement, if that can be done, and attempt to narrow down the number of places where it might be found."

One of the security men said, a little belligerently, "Doctor, just how are we supposed to find an invisible entity?"

Mookherji struggled to keep impatience out of his voice. "The visible spectrum isn't the only sort of electromagnetic energy in the universe. If this thing is alive, it's got to be radiating *somewhere* along the line. You've got a master computer with a million sensory pickups mounted all over the hospital. Can't you have the sensors scan for a point-source of infrared or ultraviolet moving through a room? Or even X rays, for God's sake: we don't know where the radiation's likely to be. Maybe it's a gamma emitter, even. Look, something wild is loose in this building, and we can't see it, but the computer can. Make it search."

Dr. Bailey said, "Perhaps the energy we ought to be trying to trace it by is, ah, telepathic energy, Doctor."

Mookherji shrugged. "As far as anybody knows, telepathic impulses propagate somewhere outside the electromagnetic spectrum. But of course you're right that I might be able to pick up some kind of output, and I intend to make a floor-by-floor search as soon as this briefing session is over." He turned toward Nakadai. "Lee, what's the word from your quarantined spacemen?"

"All six went through eight-hour sleep periods today without any sign of a nightmare episode: some dreaming, but all of it normal. In the past couple of hours I've had them on the phone talking with some of the patients who had the nightmares, and everybody agrees that the kind of dreams people have been having here today are the same in tone, texture, and general level of horror as the ones the men had aboard the ship. Images of bodily destruction and alien landscapes, accompanied by an overwhelming, almost intolerable, feeling of isolation, loneliness, separation from one's own kind."

"Which would fit the hypothesis of an alien being as the cause," said Martinson of the psychology staff. "If it's wandering around trying to communicate with us, trying to tell us it doesn't want to be here, say, and its communications reach human minds only in the form of frightful nightmares—"

"Why does it communicate only with sleeping people?" an intern asked.

"Perhaps those are the only ones it can reach. Maybe a mind that's awake isn't receptive," Martinson suggested.

"Seems to me," a security man said, "that we're making a whole lot of guesses based on no evidence at all. You're all sitting around talking about an invisible telepathic thing that breathes nightmares in people's ears, and it might just as easily be a virus that attacks the brain, or something in yesterday's food, or—"

Mookherji said, "The ideas you're offering now have already been examined and discarded. We're working on this line of inquiry now because it seems to hold together, fantastic though it sounds, and because it's all we have. If you'll excuse me, I'd like to start checking the building for telepathic output, now." He went out, pressing his hands to his throbbing temples.

14.

Satina Ransom stirred, stretched, subsided. She looked up and saw the dazzling blaze of Saturn's rings overhead, glowing through the hotel's domed roof. She had never seen anything more beautiful in her life. This close to them, only about 750,000 miles out, she could clearly make out the different zones of the rings, each revolving about Saturn at its own speed, with the blackness of space visible through the open places. And Saturn itself, gleaming in the heavens, so bright, so huge—

What was that rumbling sound? Thunder? Not here, not on Titan. Again: louder. And the ground swaying. A crack in the dome! Oh, no, no, no, feel the air rushing out, look at that cold greenish mist pouring in—people falling down all over the place—what's happening, what's happening, what's happening? Saturn seems to be falling toward us. That taste in my mouth—oh—oh —oh—

Satina screamed. And screamed. And went on screaming as she slipped down into darkness, and pulled the soft blanket of unconsciousness over her, and shivered, and gave thanks for finding a safe place to hide.

15.

Mookherji had plodded through the whole building, accompanied by three security men and a couple of interns. He had seen whole sectors of the hospital that he didn't know existed. He had toured basements and sub-basements and sub-sub-basements; he had been through laboratories and computer rooms and wards and exercise chambers. He had kept himself in a state of complete telepathic receptivity throughout the trek, but he had detected nothing, not even a flicker of mental current anywhere. Somehow that came as no surprise to him. Now, with dawn near, he wanted nothing more than sixteen hours or so of sleep. Even with nightmares. He was tired beyond all comprehension of the meaning of tiredness.

Yet something wild was loose, still, and the nightmares still were going on. Three incidents, ninety minutes apart, had occurred during the night: two patients on the fifth level and one on the sixth had awakened in states of terror. It had been possible to calm them quickly, and apparently no lasting harm had been done; but now the stranger was close to Mookherji's neuropathology ward, and he didn't like the thought of exposing a bunch of mentally unstable patients to that kind of stimulus. By this time, the control center had reprogrammed all patient-monitoring systems to watch for the early stages of nightmare—hormone changes, EEG tremors, respiration-rate rise, and so forth—in the hope of awakening a victim before the full impact could be felt. Even so, Mookherji wanted to see that thing caught and out of the hospital before it got to any of his own people.

But how?

As he trudged back to his sixth-level office, he considered some of the ideas people had tossed around in that midnight briefing session. *Wandering around trying to communicate with us,* Martinson had said. *Its communications reach human minds only in the form of frightful nightmares. Maybe a mind that's awake isn't receptive.* Even the mind of a human telepath, it seemed, wasn't receptive while awake. Mookherji wondered if he should go to sleep and hope the alien would reach him, and then try to deal with it, lead it into a trap of some kind—but no. He wasn't that different from other people. If he slept, and the alien did open contact, he'd simply have a hell of a nightmare and wake up, with nothing gained. That wasn't the answer. Suppose, though, he managed to make contact with the alien through the mind of a nightmare victim—someone he could use as a kind of telepathic loudspeaker, someone who wasn't likely to wake up while the dream was going on—

Satina.

Perhaps. Perhaps. Of course, he'd have to make sure the girl was shielded from possible harm. She had enough horrors running free in her head as it was. But if he lent her his strength, drained off the poison of the nightmare, took the impact himself via their telepathic link, and was able to stand the strain and still speak to the alien mind—that might just work. Might.

He went to her room. He clasped her hand between his.

—*Satina?*

—*Morning so soon, Doctor?*

—*It's still early, Satina. But things are a little unusual here today. We need your help. You don't have to if you don't want to, but I think you can be of great value to us, and maybe even to yourself. Listen to me very carefully, and think it over before you say yes or no—*

God help me if I'm wrong, Mookherji thought, far below the level of telepathic transmission.

16.

Chilled, alone, growing groggy with dismay and hopelessness, the Vsiir had made no attempts at contact for several hours now. What was the use? The results were always the same when it touched a human mind; it was exhausting itself and apparently bothering the humans, to no purpose. Now the sun had risen. The Vsiir contemplated slipping out of the building and exposing itself to the yellow solar radiation while dropping all defenses; it would be a quick death, an end to all this misery and longing. It was folly to dream of seeing the home planet again. And—

What was that?

A call. Clear, intelligible, unmistakable. *Come to me.* An open mind somewhere on this level, speaking neither the human language nor the Vsiir language, but using the wordless, universally comprehensible communion that occurs when mind speaks directly to mind. *Come to me. Tell me everything. How can I help you?*

In its excitement the Vsiir slid up and down the spectrum, emitting a blast of infrared, a jagged blurt of ultraviolet, a lively blaze of visible light, before getting control. Quickly it took a fix on the direction of the call. Not far away: down this corridor, under this door, through this passage. *Come to me.* Yes. Yes. Extending its mind-probes ahead of it, groping for contact with the beckoning mind, the Vsiir hastened forward.

17.

Mookherji, his mind locked to Satina's, felt the sudden crashing shock of the nightmare moving in, and even at second remove the effect was stunning in its power. He perceived a clicking sensation of mind touching mind. And then, into Satina's receptive spirit, there poured—

A wall higher than Everest. Satina trying to climb it, scrambling up a smooth white face, digging fingertips into minute crevices. Slipping back one yard for every two gained. Below, a rolling pit, flames shooting up, foul gases rising, monsters with needle-sharp fangs waiting for her to fall. The wall grows taller. The air is so thin—she can barely breathe, her eyes are dimming, a greasy hand is squeezing her heart, she can feel her veins pulling free of her flesh like wires coming out of a broken plaster ceiling, and the gravitational pull is growing constantly—pain, her lungs crumbling, her face sagging hideously—a river of terror surging through her skull—

—*None of it is real, Satina. They're just illusions. None of it is really happening.*

—*Yes,* she says, *yes, I know.* But still she resonates with fright, her muscles jerking at random, her face flushed and sweating, her eyes fluttering beneath the lids. The dream continues. How much more can she stand?

—*Give it to me,* he tells her. *Give me the dream!*

She does not understand. No matter. Mookherji knows how to do it. He is so tired that fatigue is unimportant; somewhere in the realm beyond collapse he finds unexpected strength, and reaches into her numbed soul, and pulls the hallucinations forth as though they were cobwebs. They engulf him. No longer does he experience them indirectly; now all the phantoms are loose in his skull, and, even as he feels Satina relax, he braces himself against the onslaught of unreality that he has summoned into himself. And he copes. He drains the excess of irrationality out of her and winds it about his consciousness, and adapts, learning to live with the appalling flood of images. He and Satina share what is coming forth. Together they can bear the burden; he carries more of it than she does, but she does her part, and now neither of them is overwhelmed by the parade of bogeys. They can laugh at the dream-monsters, they can even admire them for being so richly fantastic. That beast with a hundred heads, that bundle of living copper wires, that pit of dragons, that coiling mass of spiky teeth—who can fear what does not exist?

Over the clatter of bizarre images Mookherji sends a coherent thought, pushing it through Satina's mind:

—*Can you turn off the nightmares?*

—*No,* something replies. *They are in you, not in me. I only provide the liberating stimulus. You generate the images.*

—*All right. Who are you, and what do you want here?*

—*I am a Vsiir.*

—*A what?*

—*Native life-form of the planet where you collect the greenfire branches. Through my own carelessness I was transported to your planet.* Accompanying the message is an overriding impulse of sadness, a mixture of pathos, self-pity, discomfort, exhaustion. Above this the nightmares still flow, but they are insignificant now. The Vsiir says, *I wish only to be sent home. I did not want to come here.*

And this is our alien monster? Mookherji thinks. This is our fearsome, nightmare-spreading beast from the stars?

—*Why do you spread hallucinations?*

—*This was not my intention. I was merely trying to make mental contact. Some defect in the human receptive system, perhaps—I do not know. I do not know. I am so tired, though. Can you help me?*

—*We'll send you home, yes,* Mookherji promises. *Where are you? Can you show yourself to me? Let me know how to find you, and I'll notify the starport authorities, and they'll arrange for your passage home on the first ship out.*

Hesitation. Silence. Contact wavers and perhaps breaks.

—*Well?* Mookherji says, after a moment. *What's happening? Where are you?*

From the Vsiir an uneasy response:

—*How can I trust you? Perhaps you merely wish to destroy me. If I reveal myself—*

Mookherji bites his lip in sudden fury. His reserve of strength is almost gone; he can barely sustain the contact at all. And if he now has to find some way of persuading a suspicious alien to surrender itself, he may run out of steam before he can settle things. The situation calls for desperate measures.

—*Listen, Vsiir. I'm not strong enough to talk much longer, and neither is this girl I'm using. I invite you into my head. I'll drop all defenses: if you can look at who I am, look hard, and decide for yourself whether you can trust me. After that it's up to you. I can help you get home, but only if you produce yourself right away.*

He opens his mind wide. He stands mentally naked.

The Vsiir rushes into Mookherji's brain.

18.

A hand touched Mookherji's shoulder. He snapped awake instantly, blinking, trying to get his bearings. Lee Nakadai stood above him. They were in—where?—Satina Ransom's room. The pale light of early morning was coming through the window; he must have dozed only a minute or so. His head was splitting.

"We've been looking all over for you, Pete," Nakadai said.

"It's all right now," Mookherji murmured. "It's all all right." He shook his head to clear it. He remembered things. Yes. On the floor, next to Satina's bed, squatted something about the size of a frog, but very different in shape, color, and texture from any frog Mookherji had ever seen. He showed it to Nakadai. "That's the Vsiir," Mookherji said. "The alien terror. Satina and I made friends with it. We talked it into showing itself. Listen, it isn't happy here, so will you get hold of a starport official fast, and explain that we've got an organism here that has to be shipped back to Norton's Star at once, and—"

Satina said, "Are you Dr. Mookherji?"

"That's right. I suppose I should have introduced myself when—*you're awake?*"

"It's morning, isn't it?" The girl sat up, grinning. "You're younger than I thought you were. And so serious-looking. And I *love* that color of skin. I—"

"You're awake?"

"I had a bad dream," she said. "Or maybe a bad dream within a bad dream—I don't know. Whatever it was, it was pretty awful, but I felt so much better when it went away—I just felt that if I slept any longer I was going to miss a lot of good things, that I had to get up and see what was happening in the world—do you understand any of this, Doctor?"

Mookherji realized his knees were shaking. "Shock therapy," he muttered. "We blasted her loose from the coma—without even knowing what we were doing." He moved toward the bed. "Listen, Satina, I've been up for about a million years, and I'm ready to burn out from overload. And I've got a thousand things to talk about with you, only not now. Is that okay? Not now. I'll send Dr. Bailey in—he's my boss—and after I've had some sleep I'll come back and we'll go over everything together, okay? Say, five, six this evening. All right?"

"Well, of course, all right," Satina said, with a twinkling smile. "If you feel you really have to run off, just when I've—sure. Go. Go. You look awfully tired, Doctor."

Mookherji blew her a kiss. Then, taking Nakadai by the elbow, he headed for the door. When he was outside he said, "Get the Vsiir over to your quarantine place pronto and try to put it in an atmosphere it finds comfortable. And arrange for its trip home. I'll go talk to Bailey—and then I'm going to drop."

Nakadai nodded. "You get some rest, Pete. I'll handle things."

Mookherji shuffled slowly down the hall toward Dr. Bailey's office, thinking of the smile on Satina's face, thinking of the sad little Vsiir, thinking of nightmares—

"Pleasant dreams, Pete," Nakadai called.